GENE CARY

Beginnings

Stories, Poems, Anecdotes

Enjoy!
Gene Cary

First edition

ISBN: 9781735685304

Editing by Christopher Hazle-Cary

This book was professionally typeset on Reedsy.
Find out more at reedsy.com

Dedicated to my wife Jan and our children, whom I love dearly.

"Live as if you were to die tomorrow. Learn as if you were to live forever."

MAHATMA GANDHI

Contents

II   Poems and Anecdotes

Acknowledgement

I would like to acknowledge the dedicated work of the Editor, my grandson Christopher, without whom this book would not have been possible.

Editor Acknowledgement

I, the Editor, would like to thank everyone who contributed to the making of this book - firstly Grandpa Gene for the work he put in during a difficult time. Thanks also to Grandma Jan for her help, to Bruce and Allison for theirs, and to my dear friend Rena for her artistic consultation. Finally, thanks to Mom and Dad for their support, trust, and forbearance, without which I would not be in the position to take on challenging and rewarding projects like this one.

I

Stories

Zach

The wind died to a whisper. The moist air felt like what you breathe before a storm. I was on Lake Erie near Buffalo with my friend Zach. We'd often paddled there—hugging the shore, never venturing far out, never straight across like we did now. I wiped away the relentless sweat clouding my vision and looked over my shoulder at the hazy shore we'd just left. My Harley was parked next to Zach's, barely visible. The opposite shore lay undefined under a metallic sky. I glanced at the sun, unable to judge its paleness.

"We've gotta take off these damned life jackets," Zach told me. "It's too hot to wear these stuffy things."

I turned and frowned, but said nothing, used to having Zach act like the in-charge adult even though he was only a year older. It had been this way since middle school, when he protected me from bullies. It bothered me. I needed to grow up, not disguise my doubts.

"No storm's coming up," said Zach. "It's stayed clear."

Zach pointed his paddle towards widely-scattered clouds. I peered at the horizon, shrugged, and dropped my life jacket on top of Zach's in the canoe's midsection.

"How far to the other side, Zach?"

"Canada is miles from here, straight across. We'll get out a ways, then turn back."

Zach began thrusting his paddle into oncoming waves, drawing us

3

into a competitive rhythm, blocking out our awareness of a darkening sky.

"Paddle faster!" he shouted.

Lightning bounced across thickened clouds at the far end of the lake, driving the wind towards us, the broadening waves rocking the canoe.

"We ought to turn back, Zach."

"Keep paddling!"

The wind picked up, bringing in clean air that wafted away the off-shore dead fish smell. A thin froth formed on the swelling waves. The canoe pitched a few degrees steeper into them. Thunder rumbled.

I spun around to Zach. "That's it, Zach. Time to turn around."

"Not yet." Zach, his paddle in mid-stroke, cocked his head. "You afraid you can't handle it?"

"Those waves are only going to get bigger. You know how this lake is."

"Dammit, not yet!"

"What do you want to do, Zach, go clear across?" I craned back to see Zach, his face remote, as though he wasn't in it. The canoe bucked into a deeper trough.

"Zach?"

"You're so freaking smart in school, good with computers, but a dumbass when it comes to things going on around you."

I hated being sized up as a bookworm, or worse yet a geek—that's why I hooked up with Zach and his indifference to school in the first place. My father had always been buried in his lawyering, so when he wanted me to be smart, get ready for college, I wasn't. When my grades slipped he about had a shit hemorrhage. He was relieved when he heard that Zach, in his eyes always the bad influence, planned to drop out of school, enlist as a seventeen year old.

"How's Traci nowadays?" his smile was much too innocent.

"What are you talking about, Zach?" I managed to say.

4

I knew who he was talking about and he knew I knew. But I never shared with Zach, as I usually did about girls, that eye-fucking with Traci had led to steady dating, that I thought she had a yen for me. Traci—blonde hair, willowy hips, smartness that she didn't try to one-up me with, and a little bit of a lisp she called her "baby talk"—fascinated me.

"You really like broads like that don't you?"

"Just somebody at the moment," I said, turning towards Zach, hoping my disinterest showed.

"You like them smart, don't you?"

"Just a distraction. Variety, you know," I said, still trying to pass off his remark.

"Yeah, I bet! You really like to talk about things but skip the action," said Zach, pushing his paddle deeper into the water with every other word. "Maybe you can't handle the hot chicks. How about that?"

"What are you getting at, Zach?" I wanted to wipe the shit-eating smirk off his face.

"I've been seeing her."

"What? Traci?"

"She just couldn't resist. She dates other guys but only gives in to me," said Zach, his eyes measuring, amused. "Frankly, I'm not sure she's worth that much."

Zach had a masterly approach to girls which I envied—his choice at any given time was a game of roulette. But why Traci, not worth it as he declared?

"In fact, I knocked her up." Zach slammed his paddle across the canoe's gunwales.

"You bastard!"

"You don't know how to handle a canoe let alone somebody like Traci." Zach licked his lips, savoring his betrayal.

I rose, my voice stuck in the hollow of my throat, but fell back in the swaying canoe with a tight grip on the paddle I wanted to use as a cleaver. I pictured Zach toppling in the water from multiple blows, blood streaming from his head.

"I want to kill you, but I can't in this asshole of a storm." I lay sprawled out in the canoe, impotent, imagining the bashings inflicted and warded off. "You are really screwed up!" I looked up at Zach, who still steered the canoe as it twisted between the waves. "You bring me all the way out here on this lake that sucks in the first place, but even worse, we get caught in this storm. *And* you wanted to keep going because you want to tell me…" I cringed and changed position to relieve the pain that lingered from being slammed on my back by the bucking canoe. "Man, you are totally fucked up. You have a stable of girlfriends. Why in hell did you have to steal mine?"

"I already told you. She just couldn't resist."

"Bullshit! Are you sure she's pregnant?"

"Oh yeah."

"You've lied to me before."

"Yeah, I know. But right now you'd better use that paddle to help keep us from capsizing."

Electrified air bristled my hair. I moved around to the bow and grabbed the sides of the canoe to pull myself up so I could paddle. Jagged fingers of light plumbed the nearby sky, followed by a thumping crackle that pressed the air hard against me. The air filled with a burnt match smell. Thunder strummed.

Wordlessly, we headed the canoe into the oncoming waves to prevent capsizing. Minutes later, wind blew rain at a slant, cutting across our vision. Raindrops mutated into icy pellets that ricocheted inside the canoe like hard-thrown marbles and raised bee-sting welts on our skin. Waves surged to sharper heights, threatening to spin the canoe between them—a toy kicked into the corner by a jealous sibling. Thoughts of Traci's pregnancy lay dormant in my mind, hard to believe.

"We've got to keep heading…," shouted Zach.

"What?" Thunder drowned out Zach's voice.

"… swamping…," came Zach's fragmented reply.

The canoe pitched up with each wave and suspended for a moment at the crest before making a sickening slow-motion drop into the following trough. My arm froze on the paddle, disconnected from the task of guiding and propelling. I told myself to use the paddle. But how? It felt like swishing a toothpick through pulsating mud.

The thought hit me as I reached for the life jacket I'd discarded, pulling it as tightly around me as possible: Zach couldn't get us out of this mess anymore than I could. We would have to wait out the storm together, at the mercy of a lake gone mad.

I drove the paddle deep into the side of another rogue wave. The canoe made a sweep upward followed by a wrenching pitch downward. Panic seized me, reaching out to squeeze me so I couldn't breathe. I stifled the urge to throw up. I was dizzy, and realized I was holding my breath. I counted waves to fight back the deadening loss of control and the eerie vastness of a lake trying to swallow us. But I gave up and labored silently with Zach, my attention obliterated from anything but the water coming at us, time put on hold by endless waves.

Sensation returned to my arms. I dug the paddle deeper and encountered less resistance.

"Zach, we've got a chance to turn the canoe." I heard my voice crack. Zach didn't answer.

I flicked around to see Zach's eyes fixed in his face like immoveable discs.

"Zach?"

"Yeah. Gotta get it turned around," said Zach, his voice flat, spiritless.

The canoe willed its own coming about to face the next upward sweep of a wave. The next descent careened the canoe broadside into the following crest. The canoe teetered, swung downward, and then heaved over, plunging us out. The chilly Canadian water sucked away my breath and tore off the life jacket I'd managed to grab. A piston of water penetrated my nose and stabbed through to the back of my head. I watched, helpless, as the waves carried away the life jacket. What the hell was I thinking when I discarded it earlier?

The half-submerged canoe whirled on the back of the next wave and whacked me as I came up, swallowing water and gulping a bolus of air. I fell back sputtering, the sour taste of blood in my mouth. The world turned gray. My vision narrowed. I fought going limp as I sank in the water. I saw an entrance to a tunnel rushing away from me. Or was I rushing away from it, away from a spot of daylight, stepping outside my body into another time? I began to kick, flailing my arms and squirming toward the surface. An elephant must've stepped on my chest. I pushed through to the surface, my arms rubbery, and gulped a ballooned mixture of air and water that stuck in my throat. Unable to breathe, I descended again.

Suddenly, I burst through to the surface, regurgitating water.

"Zach! Zach!" I went under again but didn't sink as far. I fought to the surface once more and treaded on the up-and-down surface of the water, catching my breath. "Where are you, man? Where the hell are you?"

A wave elevated me so I could see Zach, the swamped canoe bobbing between us. I swam toward the canoe and looked over it to see Zach clutching the orange life jacket. I needed to get to him fast!

I pushed away from the canoe moored in the water like a belly up dead fish.

Zach looked groggy when I reached him. His eyes shot open. "Jesus, man! Where've you been?" He choked and sputtered water from his mouth.

"You got clipped by the canoe!"

Zach's eyes fluttered, a questioning wrinkle on his face. "Yeah. I guess

8

I was out of it for a minute."

"A minute my ass! You've been clinging to the only damned life jacket left, which you had us stow away, remember?" I pulled the life jacket around him, unable to fasten it in the choppy water. "Yeah, you were out of it all right."

I hung onto Zach and together we continued our cork-like movements as the storm's center moved past us, its violence used up. The rain softened to a velvet mist. The wind dwindled to a light breeze.

"Zach, we've got to get back to the canoe. Can you make it?" The canoe floated nearby, its bloated condition had slowed its retreat from us.

"You kidding?" It was the old overconfident Zach who talked, the one I was used to.

We swam to the idled canoe, gliding with the waves, and clung to it, mute and exhausted.

The lake became calm as we regained our strength. Neither one of us spoke. "Zach, let's turn the canoe over." Zach knew how, he'd taught me. He nodded sullenly.

Near shore an hour later, the usual fishy odor had been washed away, replaced by a cleansed-land smell and a crystal-clear sky.

Zach broke the silence once we reached the sandbar. "I'll probably enlist. I've had enough of this burg."

"What about Traci?"

"What about her?"

"What about her pregnancy?" Throbbing anger clawed at my throat.

"It's my damned kid, but she's not going to have anything to do with me! I'm only somebody along the lakeshore near the railroad tracks, not an ace like you."

Zach grinned a sheepish grin, unlike him. "I'll probably get my balls cut off by some Iraqi, but they'll have to catch me first."

Zach's lopsided grin had a touch of grimness about it. It sounded like a death wish. I didn't know how to respond. "You think it's funny, a big frigging joke, don't you?"

Zach thrust out his lower lip, opened his mouth, about to say something, when a bellow from shore interrupted him.

"Hey!" Jake, Zach's older brother, stood on shore in cutoff khakis, looking stormy and pumping his arms for us to come onto the shore.

We beached the canoe near Jake, scraping it across the uncluttered sandbar created by the storm. Jake exchanged a blank look with me, saying nothing until I started walking away across the rain-soaked sand. I could hear him swearing as he questioned Zach about the loss of the paddles and the life jacket. There was no concern about how we almost lost our lives.

I glanced back and marveled at the appearance of the two brothers as they stood facing each other. Zach's abundant dark hair, even features, and medium height—at odds with Jake's height, angular features, and reddish fringe of hair—made me wonder whether they were really brothers.

I pushed my feet into the packed sand and felt it squeeze solidly between my toes.

"Hey! Where you going in such a big hurry?" yelled Zach.

I sensed a direction, just didn't think I'd always know where. I didn't answer and kept walking—what Zach had to say was irrelevant. I clambered up the shaky stairs, not looking back, heard bits of shale slipping from its insecure hold on the cliff.

I grabbed my jacket, shoved my beach clothes into the satchel, pulled on my cycle boots and helmet, and mounted my Harley. I kicked in the starter with extra gas, feeling the strength of surging vibrations, in control and with a sense of freedom I'd never felt before. I remembered I was eligible for a full license. More than eligible, as I shot out onto the main highway.

Disclosure

The aroma of leftover coffee assaulted Jeff as he listened to Felice's weekly case presentation. Jeff worked with her as a psychiatric consultant for Child Services, supervising her on difficult abuse cases.

Not a social worker in name only, Felice really cared about what happened to the needy kids who landed on Child Services' doorstep, maybe too much. Jeff sensed that the agency respected her. Envious associates wanted her to fall flat on her face.

The fluorescent lighting in the Health and Welfare building gave Felice's black hair, perfect oval face, and almond eyes a gray sheen. She finished, and another social worker got up to speak. From one end of the formica table Felice peered at Jeff over her cat glasses.

After the meeting, Jeff sat alone in the hallway phoning his office. Felice hurried toward him holding something out in front of her between her finger and thumb, all but wrinkling her nose.

Finishing his phone call, Jeff looked up. She handed him a letter. "Felice, what's this for?"

"Read it," she demanded. "Please." Jeff's eyebrows climbed up his forehead. "I can't give you all the details now. Give me a call."

Jeff heard the plea in her voice. He shrugged, then nodded. It wasn't the first time she had laid one on him.

"It's an abuse case, a tough one," said Felice. She spun around and started down the hall, heels clicking on the marbled floor, rushed, like she didn't want to wait around for him to object.

After his last patient that evening, he slid the letter from his briefcase and read it again. *"I don't know who you think you are lady but Billy is my kid and belongs with my wife. I can get things done even if I'm in prison."*

The patchwork of colliding and uneven letters dwarfed the writer's illegible signature. To Jeff it meant impulsiveness and a person used to getting his own way.

Felice's line was busy. Jeff packed his pipe with his favorite blend of Virginia tobacco and swiveled his chair to pull down a book about psychopaths and their victims. Felice's line was busy an hour later. Fifteen minutes went by before Jeff impatiently phoned Felice a third time.

"You took your sweet time about it," Felice admonished when he finally reached her.

"I tried to get you earlier, line was busy," said Jeff. There was a pause. "Felice?"

"I'm sorry. I must've been on the phone with Donnie when you tried to reach me." Donnie was her teenage son. Weed. Oxys. Who knows what else.

"You've received letters like this before, Felice. Why's this one so different?"

"The guy who wrote it is doing time for child pornography. I think he's running a kiddie porno ring from prison." Felice sighed.

"Go on. How did you get involved?"

"I guess I'm a sucker for this kind of case. I got interested, so the director assigned it to me with a warning to get some supervision."

"You can get over-involved, Felice. We've talked about this before."

"The evidence they had against him wasn't strong enough. He left a trail of ruined childhoods and got off light—"

"So far I've heard assumptions and few facts," interrupted Jeff.

"Well jeez Jeff, will you wait'll I finish? I think the woman he calls his wife is under his thumb. I use the word wife loosely. They may not be married. I've interviewed her and she is like a clam's ass—watertight. She's scared. Won't meet your eyes. Jumpy like a rabbit. Constantly visits him in prison, maybe to get her orders."

"Does she admit to anything?" asked Jeff.

"Nothing. I only started getting letters after interviewing her. I figured she told him about their son's request for emancipation. He's a chronic runaway and has a history of being abused."

"Wait, how many letters have you received?"

"Several."

"How many?"

"Six."

"Have you reported them?"

"Nope. Wanted to make sure I had solid evidence this time. You know, sex toys and videos. If not, the porn ring will never get stamped out."

"Emancipation? Alleged wife? Abuse? Porn ring? This is a lot, Felice."

"Trying to get a grip on this guy's life is like grabbing at confetti."

"Felice, it's bigger than we can handle and, dammit, you've been trying to play detective."

"I'm letting you know about it, aren't I?" Felice's voice faltered and there was an unaccustomed silence.

"Felice, are you there?"

"Yeah."

"You were saying?"

"I think someone's been following me home. Same car—"

Jeff heard a muffled crash mingled with a scream.

"Felice! Are you all right?" Jeff could hear labored breathing for a few seconds, then a groan. "Felice!"

"I'm okay, trying to catch my breath. Shit! I just had that picture window replaced too."

"Felice, call the damned police. Do you hear me?"

"Christ. I hate the cops."

"Felice, is there anyone there with you?" Donnie was in and out of rehab, not home a lot.

"No."

"Where's Donnie?"

"Rehab. Oxys again."

"Look Felice, I don't like the sound of this. I'm coming over."

"Not necessary."

"Unless you have somebody in the wings to talk to about this soon, I think talking this out right now might be a good idea."

There was a pause before Felice answered. "Yeah, might be a good idea."

"I'll be right over."

As he drove he thought more about the possibility of a stalker. He barreled his Lexus down the bypass, ignoring a police cruiser crouched in a speed trap. He led it, siren blaring, to Felice's mid-city row house. Jeff saw the jagged pattern of the smashed picture window as he started to run up the sidewalk. The cop pulled up behind Jeff's Lexus, jumped out of the cruiser, and steadied his Smith and Wesson on the cruiser's hood. "Hey, you! Hands in the air!"

"Okay, officer. Please let me explain."

"Nice and easy, buddy. Come over here and place your hands over the hood of the patrol car."

"I can explain."

"Yeah, you sure have some explaining to do," said the cop as he came around the cruiser to pat Jeff down.

"I was phoning the woman living here when somebody broke her window. I think she may be in danger."

Jeff turned around to see Felice hurrying down the sidewalk. "The cavalry's here at last!" shouted Felice, her voice choked with false gaiety.

14

"All for one little brick." But her eyes slid away in answer to Jeff's skeptical look and she accepted his protective hug.

"I'm going to call for backup," said the cop. "Anyone else in there with you, lady?"

"No. Somebody threw a brick through my window about twenty minutes ago, but they left."

"Stay here," ordered the cop as he went in the front door to make a quick inspection, circled outside to the front, and waved them in.

The cop was kneeling gingerly beside the shattered glass when Felice and Jeff entered. He stood up to face Felice. "Need to file a report. You know who threw the brick, get a glimpse, or maybe suspect who might have done it?"

"No, except the car. It was a beat-up Ford Mustang." Jeff caught Felice's between-you-and-me look.

The cop went back outside to talk with the arriving backup. He returned and began writing a report about the incident. When he finished he handed a copy to Felice. "If you have further information about this incident or want to file a complaint, the station address and phone number is on this report. I'll have this area patrolled more frequently. Give us a call if you see anything suspicious," said the cop as he hitched up his gun belt.

"I will. Thank you very much," said Felice. Jeff noticed Felice's clenched fists.

The cop snapped his notebook shut, pulled out another, and began writing. "You, my friend," turning around and pointing a stubby finger at Jeff, "are charged with resisting arrest. The circumstances are mitigating, but you'll need to tell it to the judge."

He handed Jeff a citation. Jeff noticed the name Sergeant Lunney printed on the cop's shiny gold badge.

When the Sergeant left, Felice collapsed on the sofa. "I need a drink."

Jeff walked over to the portable bar. "Will Johnnie Walker do?"

"Yeah, but make it four fingers."

Jeff poured as instructed along with half as much for himself. He handed her the drink and sat down beside her.

Felice gulped half of her drink and sat back, stretching her head toward the ceiling, unable to squeeze back tears.

"That freaking bastard!"

"Do you mind telling me what's going on?" asked Jeff, tired of the game she was playing.

"I think I'm being watched."

"What do you mean, watched?"

"Just what I said, somebody's watching me. Dammit!"

Jeff waited while Felice regained her composure.

"There's a guy that's been parked opposite my house for the past week. He's probably my friend the brick-thrower. He parks there for a couple of hours in the same Ford Mustang, just as it gets dark."

"Does he get out of the car?"

"No. Just sits there. Wears a baseball cap. He looks young."

"You called the police about it yet, Felice?"

"Nope."

"Why not?" snapped Jeff.

"I thought maybe it was one of Donnie's friends at first, maybe looking for a hit or a bag of weed. I didn't want to get Donnie in any trouble."

Jeff picked up the tremor in Felice's voice. "He's clean now, Jeff. I was just on the phone trying to persuade him to stay longer in rehab. The center thinks he should extend his stay to avoid a relapse."

"So it doesn't have anything to do with Donnie. Right?"

Felice hesitated, then nodded.

"Fill me in on the felon," said Jeff.

"I pulled all kinds of strings, and finally persuaded the police to get a warrant to search his house. His wife still occupies it."

Jeff watched Felice bite precisely into her words. "It turned up stacks of child porn film under a loose floorboard. Stacks, Jeff! It was collected and brought back to the DA." Jeff felt he could hear Felice grind her teeth into a growl, a mother bear defending all the cubs in the forest.

Felice got up from the sofa to pace back and forth, gathering energy. Her eyes flashed as she condemned bureaucrats, corruption, and indifference. Tears evaporated on the hot flush of her cheeks. "Everybody sits on their ass while these kids get gagged, drugged, and set up for the perverts."

Felice collapsed next to Jeff and leaned back. She extended her arms limply along her sides. Jeff waited as she turned towards him and spoke quietly. "What do we do next? And don't look at me like that."

"I don't know," said Jeff, straightening up. "You carry on then throw everything into my lap."

"I apologize for dragging you into this, but your job description calls for sitting on your ass."

"That was pretty nasty," said Jeff, smiling.

"You will help me won't you, even though I've treated you like a mushroom—kept you in the dark and fed you bullshit?" It was her turn to smile.

"Yeah," said Jeff as he folded his arms and sighed.

"Then there's more that you need to know."

Jeff cocked his head in mock attention. "I'm all ears."

"The felon hired Massini."

"What? He's one of the best defense lawyers in the state." Jeff sat bolt upright and looked over at Felice. "Where'd he get the money?" As soon as he said it, Jeff knew the answer. "Uh-huh."

"Now you understand. This whole thing smells of an organization," said Felice. "And you know what? They've already started to squash evidence. Massini claims the porn either got planted or belonged to the previous owners."

"I can believe it," said Jeff, shaking his head.

"He'll likely be released soon, on bail, because of an appeal based on insufficient evidence to convict."

"So who do you think threw the brick?" asked Jeff. He leaned forward, rubbing his chin.

"I don't know," said Felice.

"How do we even know the felon is behind all this? And by the way, does he have a name?" added Jeff. "His name was illegible on the letter."

"Maynard Prichard."

"The name sounds familiar," said Jeff. "Yeah, he's the guy implicated in a recent prison murder. Nothing ever proved. It was a well-arranged execution."

Jeff looked up at Felice as she shot up from the sofa and threw up her hands. "He's a mastermind. That guy in the car, it's Pritchard's son!" She smacked her forehead with her hand. "I'm sure now! The son is under the control of his father, just like his mother!"

Felice whirled around, almost losing her balance, and dashed toward a pigeon-hole desk. She tiptoed over the scattered glass and pulled out a photograph. "This is a recent picture of his son, sixteen years old. I interviewed him a few weeks ago about his emancipation request." Jeff winced as Felice crunched over the broken glass to hand him the picture. "He preferred to be called Billy. He acted like a kid much younger than his age. He looked hurt, Jeff."

"Funny, he insisted I take this picture sitting on the bureau at his foster home." Felice sat down beside Jeff.

Jeff looked at the picture of a nondescript youngster with dark hair falling helter-skelter over a brooding face.

"His eyes really got to me," said Felice. "They were large and colorless. It was like peering into a vacant haunted cave when I looked into his face. He looked...what, disconnected?" Felice fought back tears. "My interview was longer than the usual one hour. He seemed to soak me up. He became alert as we talked, a sparkle in his eyes." Felice shivered as she gazed at the picture. She turned to Jeff. "When I left him it turned a switch, the light in his eyes simply went out."

Jeff shrugged, followed by a knowing nod. "If you think it was Prichard's son then you ought to inform the police, Felice."

"No, not yet."

"Felice, you've played this cat-and-mouse game long enough."

"Another two fingers of scotch please," said Felice."

Jeff gave Felice a sour look. He went to the bar and brought back the Johnnie Walker bottle. He plunked it down next to her empty glass on the coffee table.

"What harebrained idea are you hatching, Felice?"

Jeff waved no over his glass as she poured more scotch for herself. She sipped thoughtfully, her eyes fixed on the picture of Billy.

"Suppose he's under Prichard's control just like his mother and feels compelled to obey his masterminding father? That may be the reason for his request for emancipation. To follow his orders," said Felice.

"That's possible," said Jeff, remembering his refreshed knowledge of abuse. "But you're still dealing with assumptions," reminded Jeff.

"That's the point. The only way to flush out Prichard and prove he is an abuser is to catch somebody following his orders."

"I don't like it Felice. You're flirting with disaster and still acting too much like a cop."

Felice snorted, but her eyebrows began to furrow more deeply on her forehead.

A ringing telephone interrupted them and Felice went to the phone, drink in hand, to answer it.

"Thanks. No, I don't have anything to add." Felice turned to Jeff and frowned. "No other complaints."

Felice looked dazed as she hung up the phone and walked back to the sofa. "I can't believe it. They found Billy. He confessed. They took him back to his foster home and placed him on restriction."

19

"You have to hand it to their timing. How did they know it was Billy?"

"The foster home reported him missing." Felice looked puzzled. "The police said he was eager to confess." She sat down and carefully folded her hands on her lap.

"Another thing. They said his father would be released from prison soon."

"How soon is soon?"

"They didn't say exactly. Maybe a week, perhaps sooner."

Jeff felt his patience ebbing. "Look Felice, you need to go to the police before this bastard gets out of prison."

Felice nodded numbly.

"You've got to quit playing vigilante. It took having the shit scared out of you to show you that you're in over your head."

"Actually Jeff, I've been scared all along. I called my sister and asked to stay with her for a while. She lives a few miles outside the city. It's just I've seen this get buried before and—"

"I know, Felice," interrupted Jeff. "I heard you rant about it. Remember? Let the cops do their jobs. Meanwhile get packed and go live with your sister."

Felice looked deflated. "Okay Jeff, I will, if you tell the police about the meaning of the letter."

"No problem." But he did have a problem. He was thinking of his divorce two years ago—ending a childless marriage with a woman dominated by her mother. *What opposites. One as passive as the other is committed and energetic.* His strict New England conscience stifled thoughts of involvement in another relationship until the proper passage of time. But after two years he felt too locked into bachelorhood.

"Jeff, what are you thinking?"

"It might be a good idea if I stayed here tonight."

Felice frowned. "No Jeff, but thanks anyway."

Jeff could swear she tapped her foot, as though measuring the distance between them. Like a cat keeping its distance.

"I promise to move in with my sister tomorrow morning."

Jeff left Felice and returned to his bachelor quarters. She promised she would keep him updated and call the police.

In the middle of the night Jeff fumbled bleary-eyed for his ringing phone. "Jeff," Felice whispered. "Somebody is trying to break into my house. I started hearing—". The phone went dead.

"Hello! Hello!" No answer. Jeff punched 911 from the bedside stand to report a break-in. He bolted off the bed and hurriedly dressed.

For the second time within twenty-four hours Jeff sped down the bypass. Soon after he exited he saw flashing lights. *Thank God! But were they in time?*

When Jeff turned the corner, a cop bedecked in a neon vest directed him to continue straight ahead. Jeff swung the Lexus around the next corner, circled the block, and encountered another cop who also diverted him from the flashing lights. Shifting into reverse, he slipped into the nearest parking space, jumped out, and hurried up the street.

Yellow tape cordoned off Felice's row house. Jeff spotted Sergeant Lunney waving away curious onlookers. "Hello, officer."

Lunney whirled around and motioned Jeff away from the tape. "Do you recognize me, sir? I was the one with the woman this evening in her house here." Lunney scowled and turned away from the swirling lights, compressing his double chin. Recognition dawned.

"Yeah. You're the guy I chased here today." Lunney quickly wiped off a grin. "I suppose you'd like to see her?"

"Yes. Is she okay?"

"Yeah. She sure had a fright though. Don't know about the guy that got shot."

"Shot? Who got shot?"

"I don't know. There were two others besides her. Wait here, I'll see if I can get you through. I expected her to be all hysterical for a while, but she's a tough cookie. I know the type—hurt once but never again. Tougher-than-the-world type. Maybe she is, maybe she isn't. All I know is she could use a friend."

Lunney turned to his partner further down the barrier. "Hey Jake! Let this guy in. He's a friend." Jake had to be yelled at twice more before he understood. "Yeah, a friend," said Lunney, his Irish brogue less pronounced when he yelled.

Jeff got ushered by the wavering tape just as a boxy ambulance beeped through, its whirling light engulfed by multiple others. An empty body bag on a stretcher wheeled up behind Jeff.

Jeff entered and saw Felice sitting on the sofa, her face hidden behind tremulous hands.

"Felice," Jeff said softly. He sat beside her on the sofa and hugged her, rocking her gently as she crumpled against him, whimpering.

"What an asshole I am," said Felice. "I put myself in this situation and then ask everybody to rescue me." Felice continued resting against Jeff and then suddenly pulled away. Her tremors stopped as she took her hands away from her face to give him a stiff smile.

"Cripes, guy, where've you been? Don't you know the cavalry is supposed to arrive on time?" Jeff stared at her face. It was swollen and red. "Okay, what are you looking at?" Jeff startled when she pounded hard on the sofa several times. "That son of a bitch Prichard whacked me across the face!" The flush of rage made the handprint on her face stand out.

"Tell me what happened."

"You won't believe it."

"Try me."

"Well, Maynard Prichard wanted me dead. I think he finally snapped."

22

Jeff sensed wariness in her ability to stay calm as she looked away.

"Oh Jeff, he is one scary dude. He's got those eyes that bug out when he's mad. And God, was he mad!" Felice turned back to Jeff and shook her head.

"He told me nobody gets in his way, and that I was a pretty smart broad to figure out what was going on." Felice's voice trailed off. "That's when he backhanded me. Oh, what a backhand!" said Felice, turning away and fighting back tears.

"You don't have to talk anymore about this now, Felice." When he reached over to hold her hand, she snatched it away.

"Dammit, I want to. Yeah, and Billy is his son. He beat his chest like King Kong about that!" Felice's dark eyes brightened with anger.

"He said that Billy was supposed to kill me and that he, Maynard, was going to make sure he did it this time. And there was Billy standing next to him. Next to him, Jeff!"

"Billy didn't say a word the whole time. You see, Billy had other ideas." Jeff saw her hands shaking again as she paused, a diver coming up for air before the next dive underwater.

"When Maynard handed Billy the gun—" Felice shuddered, "Billy just reached across and pointed it at Maynard's head." Felice pointed to her forehead with her index finger.

Jeff looked around, bewildered. There was no sign of a struggle, blood, or somebody's brains smeared on the wall.

"Yeah," Felice nodded. "Don't be looking around here for a mess. Try the kitchen."

Jeff gave Felice a wry smile when Felice looked up at him, her face cupped in both hands. "How about another drink. I could really use it," said Felice.

"You know Felice, I wish you'd trade those glasses in for a rimless pair. You look too much like a damned cat with them."

"Cats are independent, you know. That's me," said Felice.

23

The Ring

"Gina took off for California," said the bartender as he wiped away the residue left by wet glasses and set the topped-off Yuengling next to the poured shot. Hunter wanted to reach across the bar and rip out the bartender's tongue.

Hunter downed the whiskey with half the Yuengling, bought a six-pack, and headed out to his Harley. He shoved the six-pack into the satchel and gunned the motorcycle out of the potholed parking lot onto the macadam.

Numbing vibrations shot up his arm as he sped along the lake road until he spotted an inlet, once a launch spot for his friend Zach's canoe. He veered off and skidded to a stop, popped open a Yuengling, and propped himself against the Harley to drink it.

* * *

Only two months earlier—a lifetime ago—he had met Gina at this same bar, a hangout for bikers and college-break kids, located along the Lake Erie shore near Buffalo. It was one of Zach's favorites, and Hunter had wanted to be alone to grieve Zach's recent IED death in Iraq.

As his thoughts circled around to his loneliness, he banged the beer glass down hard on the bar. He needed to take charge of his life, settle down.

The name "Lakeside" arched across the picture window in chipped silver letters and glittered through frayed curtains with each lightning flash from a summer storm. He ignored comments coming from the earlier-than-usual happy hour crowd and stayed huddled over his drink.

Thunder rattled the windows, and when Hunter jerked up he saw a young woman sitting next to him. He didn't recognize her at first and gave her a bug off look. He resumed his gloomy vigil until unable to ignore the insistent jostling of her elbow.

"Who the hell are you?" Hunter asked.

"Huh. Maybe if you turned around you'd find out," said the woman.

He squinted in the back-bar mirror to meet her gaze, skewered by her dark eyes.

"I heard about Zach. It's tough to have a friend killed...But shit happens."

Her direct manner had prodded his memory.

"Yeah, it's me, Gina." She swept back a curtain of her dark hair with a deft finger and tucked it behind one ear.

He turned to face her. "Sorry. I didn't recognize you at first. You knew Zach?" he asked.

"Did I know Zach? Did you ever notice that talking *with* Zach meant talking *about* Zach?"

Their knees almost touched. He felt as though a cloud had passed away from him and sharpened his vision. She picked up on his new found lightness and smiled with one elbow propped on the bar as she faced him. Toughness surfaced through the fragile beauty of her dusky skin.

"How did you get to know Zach?" she asked.

"Got to know him when he protected me from bullies in middle school. He was like an older brother, one I never had."

"Yeah, well I think he might've done some bullying of his own."

"How do you know that?"

"Don't get mad. I'm only saying there must've been a lot of reasons for Zach to be your buddy."

"Well, he lived down the street. We got into trouble together. The usual boyhood pranks."

"Yeah. I bet. You don't like to think he could've done anything way-out bad."

Thoughts about how Zach coaxed him out of his shyness spun in his mind, entangled with those about his father's lingering preoccupation with the cancer death of his mother. When Zach brought him into the warmth of his close-knit family he wondered why his parents ever wanted a child in the first place.

"So you are an only child?"

"Yeah."

"So what do you do?"

"Got my own electronics business. Set it up with the inheritance from my father when he died a year ago. Run it right out of my house."

"I bet you were a good student, right?"

He hated to be thought of as a bookworm, let alone a geek. That's the reason he hooked up with Zach in the first place—his indifference to school. "My parents never asked about my grades. So when they wanted me to be smart, I wasn't."

"I'm only teasing."

The tongue ring slipping around her mouth distracted him as he tried to sort out some of the high school days he might've shared with her. He remembered the mini-skirts she wore drove guys nutty and lent credibility to talk about her waywardness.

"What's on your mind?" said Gina.

"I remember the time Zach went bungee jumping off the Eden railroad bridge. I think I saw you there." An image of Gina dressed in an eye-catching skirt flashed through his mind. She'd stood at the head of a throng of onlookers egging him on. Hunter had chickened out when Zach pushed him to jump. He was no match for Zach's daredeviltry.

"Did you ever go out with him?"

"No. He was too full of bullshit for me." She tilted her head and smiled. "You're a straight arrow, aren't you? Can't take a chance."

As they continued to talk, she carried most of the conversation. Her vibrant laugh sounded like she owned the air around her, and his gloom faded as her laugh washed over him.

"How did you learn to drink like that?" Hunter asked as he nodded to the paired drinks in front of her.

"My old man taught me." She glanced down the bar at recent arrivals and returned some nods. "He liked a shot and a bump. Besides, this is a special occasion."

"Why's that?"

"I've always admired you from a distance."

"You're putting me on."

"Do you remember Ms. Borchard, the English teacher?"

"Oh yeah."

"I walked into her class one day to deliver notices."

"And so?" He could imagine Gina's saunter in the school corridors.

"She asked the class who the Son of Man was."

Hunter's memory was vague.

"Everybody gave her dumb looks but you." Gina drank the dregs of her chaser and rolled her head questioningly to one side. "Were you shy about knowing the answer was Jesus Christ when no one else did?"

"Is it important to you?"

"Christ took on other people's pain. But it wasn't enough." She looked like a serious-minded child, her chin propped between her hands.

"So you and Zach were close?"

"As I said, we'd known each other since middle school."

27

"Yeah, and I heard he knocked up your girlfriend and that's why he enlisted...took off for Iraq."

"I don't need this!"

"Sorry. I should've kept my mouth shut." Gina got up to leave.

"No. Stay." He turned half-way toward her, caught her by the wrist and studied her high cheeked face in the mirror. "I'm just too wound up." Hunter knew Zach had kept a stable of girlfriends.

"Okay, but let me buy this round."

Gina began to stagger as her trips to the toilet increased. On one return Hunter embraced her to keep her from falling, and she pressed against him before she pulled away and sat down.

"You ever been in jail?" she asked.

"No."

"Yeah, well I have." She told him about running away from home and being placed in a lockdown. She clutched at Hunter and dug her fingernails into his arm. When he reached one arm around her she leaned into him for a moment.

"Hey Gina!" shouted a voice from the other end of the bar.

"Some half-assed bikers," Gina whispered to Hunter. She turned and nodded in the direction of the voice, where three bikers drowned out normal conversation. One of them shot a look at Gina when she looked his way.

"Don't look at them until I introduce you. Just let me handle this." Gina slid off the bar stool, drink in hand, and walked to the far end of the bar. Hunter did as he was told, wondering what would happen next, alert to Gina's warning. Handle what? The drum in his chest beat faster.

"Ted, where have you been hanging out lately?" Hunter heard Gina say as she set her drink down next to Ted's and climbed up on the bar stool next to him. She turned half-way around toward Hunter sitting alone. "This is my friend, Hunter."

Hunter turned and faced the bikers. Two wore faded brown jackets studded with tarnished silver. One carried a German infantry helmet under his arm and plunked it down on the middle of the bar.

The bikers scrutinized Hunter. One grinned and cocked his head. Another pulled himself around and folded his arms across his barrel chest.

Hunter, wondering what would happen next, felt the hair on the back of his neck prickle. He forced himself to smile.

Gina turned to the bartender. "Joe, can't you use some other soap to wash glasses? God, I'll chip in for it if it means I won't be maced to death from that cheap stuff you bought from some slaughterhouse." She turned to the biker with the kraut helmet. "Max here has a sensitive nose. You'll lose him as a regular, you keep that up."

The bartender grinned, the fog of tension lifted. "Okay guys. What'll it be?"

The bikers' conversation was replaced for a moment by furtive glances around the room. The biker with an orange brush of hair leaned toward Hunter. "So your name is Hunter. Call you by any other name?"

Hunter braced for another kicker comment.

"We're all friends here," interrupted Gina.

The biker with the kraut helmet pulled his arms tight around his muscular chest, looking skeptical.

The smallest of the three bikers, his face squeezed thin like a blade, turned toward Hunter and raised his glass. "Here's to friendship and a long life." The other bikers raised their drinks as though commanded.

"Your name's Hunter. That right?" said the thin-faced one.

"Hunter, this is Jay," said Gina.

"I knew Gina in high school," said Hunter. "Just renewing our friendship."

Jay's watery gray eyes moved past Hunter. "Glad you're able to do that."

Hunter turned back to his drink. He wondered whether there was something more he should've said.

Gina's high-pitched laughter signaled her exit from the bikers' orbit. She slid back onto the bar stool next to Hunter, a stiff smile on her face.

Hunter leaned toward her. "You're good at this," he whispered.

"Like I said, I grew up in these places." She reached for her whiskey. "I used to talk my old man out of beating my mother, even took some of the beatings myself."

She banged her empty glass down on the bar. "What the hell! I'm here drinking with a guy I've always liked. Feel better about yourself. That's what Zach would've wanted. Right?"

"Even Zach didn't always know what he wanted."

"You could ask him. Do you visit his grave like some homesick calf, talk to his grave?"

"Not as often as I used to."

"Good. It's not like talking to a live body." The soft tunnel between her breasts became visible when she leaned forward. She caught his gaze when he pulled his eyes away. Hunter gave her a wry smile, not ready to forget Zach—the confidence he'd inspired, his gift for gab, his mastery with women. He felt like he was waiting for somebody to fill a void in his life, once filled by Zach. But Zach was now gone forever, no longer alive to emulate.

Hunter and Gina continued to meet at the Lakeside. The smell of day-labor sweat grew with the crowd and receded with the dampening effect of booze. She brushed her hand over the back of his when he mentioned Zach and smacked her hand on the bar to tell him to get over it. He liked her throaty laugh that turned heads. Too much of it embarrassed him. It was the way she coated her words with upbeat optimism he liked the most.

"Look," she said one night at the Lakeside. "I've got this new tongue ring." He watched her roll a silver, pea-sized ornament in the palm of

30

her hand. "It matches the other one." She opened her mouth and jabbed the barb into her tongue, unmoved by the pain.

"Why do you want to hurt yourself?" he said as he grabbed her by the wrist. The patch of blood he saw on her lips made him think of Zach, who had no choice in his IED death.

"Do you think I'm pretty?"

"Of course."

"Okay, I'll stop if you just stop talking about Zach. He isn't worth your grief." She pulled the shiny ornament out of her mouth, held it in the palm of her hand, and rolled it side-to-side. "Look, I'll even seal the deal." She flattened out his palm, placed the small globe of silver into it, and closed his hand over it. "I won't put anymore of these in my mouth, and you won't talk anymore about Zach."

The innocent-looking object, except for its bloodletting barb, felt lighter than a ball bearing. He rolled it in his hand, picked it up and held it between thumb and forefinger. He'd held marbles this way as a kid.

"We need another drink," shouted Gina.

Hunter cringed as Gina pounded on the bar for two more paired drinks. The bartender strode toward them, tight-lipped, and wiped his hands on his beer-stained apron. "We don't need any more of your dramatics around here." He jerked his thumb toward the door.

"Oh, fuck off man!"

The bartender looked toward Hunter. "Better keep her in tow buddy." The bartender moved toward other customers.

Hunter clasped Gina's hand.

"It's my body." She hammered on the bar with her free hand. "And I decide what to do with it."

"Yeah, but it still makes me wonder why you do it."

"I know that, but I told you I won't do it anymore. So smile." A frown replaced her improvised smile.

31

He didn't resist her reaching over to kiss him, even though he felt the paralysis coming from not knowing what to expect next. His lips softened before going numb. His fleeting response seemed to make her take stock, and he emphasized it with a nod toward the door.

"We need to get out of here," said Gina. She turned and stared down the upturned faces of drinkers who waited for the next turn of events.

Hunter was glad to leave. He accepted her invitation to go to her place, bought a six-pack to go, tipped the bartender a buck, and headed out the door with Gina.

They drank half of the six-pack at her kitchen table. When they stopped talking she led him to her bedroom. He pulled off his shoes, fell into her bed, and turned his head away.

In the predawn morning he got up to pee. When he returned to her bed and finished undressing he felt the flutter of bed covers as she slid in close and cuddled against him.

A morning downpour stirred the memory of Hunter's last canoe trip with Zach. He remembered Zach's war cry as they steered across the lake. The smell of seaweed and dead fish hung heavily in the air. He'd turned just as lightning lit up the sky. He saw Zach's rain-soaked hair turn a ghoulish gray. Zach laughed hysterically. "This is what hell must be like!" he shouted, just as a wave capsized them.

Hunter lay still as Gina leaned on one elbow and brushed her hand over him, his memory interrupted. He blinked sleepily as she arched across him to plant him into her and nurse him to fulfillment.

"You're the first guy who didn't want it the night before," she said through the fog of his contentment.

He saw tracks on her skin—nodular razor scars extending across her inner arm like a child's string of beads. The sleeveless babydoll nightie couldn't hide them.

"What are these?" When he reached to touch them she jumped up and hurried toward the window to sniff the rain-cleared air.

32

"Look, you don't know me. I'm damaged goods." She turned around and flashed a smile.

He knew enough to know she filled an emotional void in his life, pushing through despite her wayward ways.

"Bacon and eggs?" He felt her loose nightie brush past him, her arms folded mockingly over it like a scolding mother. "I'm good at frying bacon and eggs."

They met more often after that, not only at the Lakeside but at his place or hers.

"Look," he said to her one afternoon as they drank beer in his cramped living room, "two can live as cheap as one."

She looked around the room, cluttered with a tangle of cables, monitors, and loose hard drives waiting to be fixed up and sold. "Hah! You'd have me cleaning up this mess, a housemaid, in no time."

"We'd manage. I'd help."

"No way!"

"Your place then?"

"Would it be any different?"

Hunter realized the absurdity of his question.

Gina tipped back her beer bottle to take a long guzzle, her eyes never leaving his. "You don't get it do you? I don't want to be beaten down like my mother was." She slammed her bottle down on the table. "Let's just enjoy what we have."

One afternoon while he showered she'd burst into his bathroom. His freelance business meant she could often find him home during the day. "Look at what I brought you." When he stepped out of the shower she tossed him a towel. "See?" She dangled filmy, narrow underwear from her hand. "It's like a G-string. Now you're more likely to get laid."

"Do you think that's all I'll need in life?"

"You really ought to try it on."

He stared at her as she stretched the bikini underwear between her hands and teasingly snapped it. When he stepped toward her she stepped back in unison, rolled up one jiggling hip, and raised an eyebrow.

"Come on big guy. Try it on!"

She pushed him away when he led her into the bedroom and pounded on his chest. "Why do you have to be so damn nice to me? I can't feel anything! Slap me! Hurt me!"

"There's no way I'm going to hurt you Gina. Ever!" Bewildered, he held her in his arms. When her childlike wailing stopped he lowered her onto the bed. She thrust her body upward to pull him inside her. She clung hard to him as though trying to encompass him into some soft part of her that had broken open.

"I wish I could figure you out." They lay entwined, her tears trickling on his arm.

"There's nothing to figure out. I am what I am. You don't need to know anything more about me."

"I've asked you this before."

"What?" She raised her head to peer over at him.

"Why don't we live together?" She'd been emphatic a week ago when he asked the same question. He'd backed off then and did now when she said *"No."* Again. He didn't want their relationship tipped so far away from him that it would cease to exist.

They continued to meet regularly. When she didn't show up for a few days, Hunter suspected she might be on a binge—perhaps with someone else. When he called at the restaurant where she waitressed, he was told she was on an extended leave of absence.

A few hours later she showed up at Hunter's place, fuming, hair falling helter-skelter around her face.

34

"Where've you been?" asked Hunter.

"Drunk and disorderly, they said. Nice jails they have around here, one toilet for every dozen in a cell," said Gina.

"I've asked you before Gina—why not move in with me? Now is the time."

"I gotta get back to work." She sprang up from her chair. "Most of my good will's been used up. The boss has looked the other way about my jail time. Nice guy, my boss." She laughed and gave him a dismissive wink. "Look, I promise I'll meet you more often."

They did meet more often for two weeks, at the Lakeside, and at his place and hers, until she dropped out of sight again, unreachable at work or at her place. A week later she showed up at the Lakeside, her eyes dull and haggard. Pale skin hung puffed over the high points of her face and stretched shiny and thin over the bony surfaces of her arms.

"Yeah, I look like hell."

"Is that all you can say?"

"I'm getting help. I went to a shrink, one that I saw when I was a kid. Seems to understand. Wants me to go to AA and see him. I knew I was in trouble when I took on a second job and couldn't sleep, started drinking more. I was flying too high. Used booze to calm me down. Besides, a lot of family baggage cropped up when my father returned to visit relatives who don't want a thing to do with him, me included. A lot of bad memories."

"Are you going to keep going?"

"I plan to."

Hunter felt a frown tighten on his forehead. "Where've you been staying?"

"Oh, back off."

"Well?"

"With a friend, a girlfriend, so don't worry."

35

"Move in with me Gina."

Gina hesitated before saying, "No. Again. No."

Hunter pressed on. "Dammit Gina, when are you going to stop destroying yourself?"

"I'm trying to figure that out." Her dark eyes dimmed.

"I'm asking you again, Gina. Move in with me?"

"Okay. I'll do it. I mean why not?" She threw her hands into the air.

It surprised him that she relented unconditionally, as though she had given up a part of herself.

"We can do it now. I can move your stuff with my pickup."

"No. I've got to get it together."

"Tomorrow?"

"Yeah. I'll give you a call."

"Okay, let's drink to that."

* * *

That was the last time he saw her.

For the past three days she hadn't returned his phone calls. The bartender told him why. He was unable to concentrate on his business, often daydreaming and phoning Gina periodically. He had ridden his Harley more often to the lake, like a compass pointing north.

One evening he parked the Harley at Zach's launch spot near some tall junipers where he could see the road and not be seen. He pulled out a Yuengling from the satchel and uncapped it.

The sound of motorcycles startled him. He turned toward the road as they roared by, led by the thin-faced Jay and flanked by Ted, a turned-around baseball cap clamped on his head. Raven-black hair streamed from the rider who held tight to Ted. Gina! "Motherfuckers!" howled

36

Hunter against the earsplitting din that sucked away every sound but its own.

After midnight Hunter kicked in the Harley's starter and rode to the Lakeside. He parked the cycle, pulled out a Yuengling, and turned around to the window marked "Lakeside." He hefted the amber-colored bottle. It felt like the dead weight of the past. His mad-dog anger spurred him on as he turned and arched his arm back to hurl it crashing into the window.

Something jabbed Hunter's side as he turned around. He slipped the unused Yuengling back into the satchel, reached into his pocket and pulled out the tongue ring. He held it in his hand, weighed it, and shifted it from one hand to the other, feeling a soothing effect wrapped in pain.

Intermission

The thick Sarasota air was like what one breathes before a storm. I wanted to return inside the Asolo to be buffeted by the air conditioning. I also wanted to relieve my curiosity. Could it be Rebecca? Flashing eyes enhanced by tanned skin and dark hair gave her a familiar appearance. She looked beautiful, but in a hardened way—her gleaming, bejeweled fingers waving at people she knew but wouldn't approach, like a woman for whom things were done.

I'd first met Rebecca on a double date with my fellow pre-med Bo. While Rebecca and I waited for my date to show up, Bo had lingered in the bar room. "He's probably looking for a sexpot," she said. She placed her hand on my knee as we drank affordable Yuengling and laughed at my burning cheeks as her hand wandered over my thigh. "He can go piss up a bent rope," she whispered and removed her hand as Bo returned.

Now, she stood on the shallow steps of the Asolo and singled me out with lioness eyes, nearly golden in the artificial light. It had been twenty years since I'd seen her at some University of Buffalo alumni gathering. A half smile broke across her face and her eyes darkened as I stepped toward her, continuing up the Asolo steps, wondering what I was getting into.

"Hello Peter. You do remember me after all. I prepared myself for you to forget me altogether."

She bent her head to one side, measuring me. She brushed back her well-kept hair with a deft forefinger. Unwieldy hair had always bothered her. It was now carefully streaked with gray. The taut surfaces of a well-attended, mature body had succeeded her supple roundedness—she'd always complained about her weight. If anything, she now looked a little gaunt under the artificial light.

I looked around, embarrassed, wondering whether a possessive spouse might be lurking nearby. It flashed through my mind that she loved to make her admirers jealous.

"The last time I saw you your nose was sitting over on one side of your face." She was referring to U of B's 1980 end-of-season game, when a behemoth defensive tackle had flattened me. She didn't mention that she'd visited me in the hospital while I recovered from the nose repair. She'd moved me to the end of the hall, away from the scrutiny of the nurses. She'd reached under the covers to feel me harden and worked to bring me to a climax.

"That's when I decided to turn my football in for a microscope."

"It still give you trouble?"

"At high altitudes I feel smothered." It also reminded me that my relationship with Rebecca got busted shortly after my nose did.

"So how does Texas suit you?" I asked with as much nonchalance as I could muster. A Latin scholar, she had dropped out in her junior year in order to marry into an oil-rich Texas family. I had lost track of her after that, but carried memories as well as scars of our whirlwind relationship.

"Fine." Her sideways look left me wondering. "Your daughter has one of the leads in the play tonight. McMurtry's plays are hard to pull off."

"She has a lot of talent, got trained here at the Asolo and Duke."

"You must be proud of her," said Rebecca with precise enunciation.

"Yes, I am. She's gotten a lot of encouragement." I was abrupt in reaction to her iciness.

Rebecca looked past me. I turned to see a heavyset, florid-faced man in a cream-colored suit lumber toward us. He picked his way up the stairs, his laughter contagious as he joked about his stumbling gait to a stately man I recognized as the mayor of Sarasota.

"Yeah, it's him. My lovable Texan, in the flesh. A lot of flesh." Rebecca shrugged. "It'll take him a few minutes to get up the stairs. He loves an audience." She compressed her lips like a mother about to scold a wayward child. "His name is Alex in case you've forgotten."

I never really knew.

Alex doffed his Stetson to the Mayor's wife, revealing a fringe of graying hair circling his bald head. He continued up the stairs, working the crowd, his conversation raucous, showing off the silver medallion attached to his string tie.

"I've heard a lot about your career as a cardiac surgeon in the U of B Alumni News," said Rebecca. "I'm very impressed. Your daughter must be proud of you, just like you are of her. And so must your wife." She looked around. "By the way where is she?"

"We've been separated for the past year."

"Oh I didn't know." I remembered that Rebecca often held back on what she knew.

"Well, why don't you visit us in Texas sometime and see it for yourself." She looked at me through the top of her eyes as though she had her own answer firmly in place.

"Better yet, why don't you visit us at the Ritz Carlton here in Sarasota. The Marathon Oil Company is putting on a benefit art auction at the Ritz." She stared down towards Alex extolling the virtues of Texas. "Bring your daughter." Her eyes swung steadily around to mine. "She is your only offspring?" she asked, her eyes vacant for a moment.

"Yes. By the way, how many children do you have?" I asked.

"Three, by his first marriage. They've all started their own families, but can't bear to leave Texas and their Daddy."

I caught the caustic note in her voice and hesitated.

"You're probably curious as to why I didn't have children of my own?"

"Yes, I guess I am. A South Buffalo Irish Catholic would be primed to have children."

"I've always been a wavering Catholic." She arched one eyebrow. "As you know."

"Look Rebecca, this is not a confessional and I'm not looking to pry—"

"But maybe you ought to." Her cheeks glowed through the tan, whether from anger or disappointment, I couldn't tell. She was a master at shading her feelings.

"Okay, why?"

"I'm shanty Irish, not lace curtain Irish." She smoothed her lips with the tip of her tongue. "I wanted to leave all that behind."

"And you did. You once told me over a few beers you wanted to marry a rich doctor. You just changed it to a rich oil man."

"Yeah, all those lean years. No way!"

"You could've married a doctor who was already rich." I put my hand up to shush her.

"Then he could buy anything he wanted, including another wife or a mistress on the side," she interjected. Her gaze circled the intermission crowd. She nodded to some acquaintances. "Believe it or not I value loyalty, despite my flaws."

"Well you sure kept Bo and I busy," I blurted out. "I'm sorry, I didn't mean that."

"But remember, I only slept with you two guys. Kind of like Butch Cassidy and the Sundance Kid."

It was hard to believe her two-at-a-time loyalty.

"Yeah, I was a party girl and went out with some rich fraternity guys, but I kept them in line."

She turned half-way toward Alex, now a few steps below and still caught up in animated conversation. "The two of you were buried in books." She folded her arms. "Do you remember those days?"

A moment of silence held between us.

"And as for keeping you busy—" she lowered her voice, "I eventually ended up pregnant." She looked away for a moment. "By one of you."

"What! You're lying!" Playgoers flocking back into the theater looked over their shoulders while we locked into each other's glare.

Rebecca broke through our trance with a thin smile. "Birth control pills don't always work when not taken regularly, especially by a conscience-stricken South Buffalo Catholic."

"Come to think of it, you told me you needed to find the right priest for your confessions. But dammit, you never told me you were pregnant."

"We had plenty of scares though." Rebecca grinned. "Those hot baths really worked, didn't they?"

"Yes!" The cords in my neck went taut. Memories of her delayed menstruation welled up, making me blush. Rebecca's face bloomed when I looked up at her from a step below. I felt a sheepish grin on my face as she looked down towards me.

"Do you remember when I dropped out of U of B for a few weeks? "Yes."

"I had an abortion. It was a tubal pregnancy. That and endometriosis led to infertility. Alex is ten years older and has fertility problems of his own, but we've tried." I wondered whether she wanted me to feel some of the pain she must've felt.

Rebecca's face stiffened as she looked down the steps. "Alex! Over here." She waved to Alex as he came toward us. He almost tripped over the last step. "I want you to meet a friend of mine."

"Yep, sure Becky."

"This is the doctor I told you about, the one I knew in college. Peter Horby. Remember?"

"Pleased to meet ya," said Alex, his drawl less intense with a smaller audience than a few moments ago. "Yes, I believe you've mentioned

42

this gentleman, yes indeed." Alex gripped my hand with his sweaty one just as the recall light blinked. "Best we go in, love."

"Alex, I'd like to invite Peter to the art auction benefit at the Ritz Carlton next Monday."

"Of course."

"His daughter is in the play here tonight. Do you remember? I pointed out her name in the program."

"Oh, do tell. Talented young lady," said Alex, without acknowledging what part Emily took.

Rebecca walked into the foyer with Alex not far behind. "Be sure to invite Emily."

"Absolutely. When? Where?"

"Come to the Presidential Suite. Oh, let's say 6 p.m.—before the crowd gets there. We can talk before going to the auction." She winked at me. "I know it'll be okay for Emily because Asolo is dark on Mondays. Right?"

I beat back the wave of anticipation warming my cheeks. Could she see it?

* * *

After the play I met Emily at the stage door and we went to the Café Bijou as I had promised.

"Dad, this place is great!" said Emily as she read the menu.

"I suggest the Escargot and the Horseradish-Encrusted Grouper."

"You sound like you've been here before."

"Yes, one time with your mother."

"Then that's as good a recommendation as I could have." Emily sat back and pretended to study her menu. Without looking up she said, "I

43

talked with Mom today. She sounded great."

I glanced at Emily and studied the high cheekbones and close-cropped blonde hair that so resembled her Mother's good looks. Incredibly, her pale blue eyes and quick captivating smile mimicked Rebecca's.

"Dad, you act as though you're mesmerized."

"No. Just thinking about the play. Somebody told me a McMurtry play is hard to pull off. Is it?"

"McMurtry is passionate and looks at all the possibilities in life. You have to enter into your role in an honest way." Emily frowned and I felt caught.

"I'm glad your mother is doing okay. But I think you two have been conspiring." I forced a smile as Emily leaned forward.

"Dad, you all right?" Emily leaned on the table, her face propped between her hands.

"Yeah."

"Sure?" She spread the menu on the table in a matter-of-fact gesture so much like her mother's. "No, I'm not conspiring." I heard an angry edge in her voice as she added, "It's just that I think you two are made for each other despite your differences."

"Viva la difference," I said, trying to break free from the painful scrutiny of my broken marriage.

"She loves you, Dad, really. Just doesn't know how to get back to you. Both of you are so stubborn."

"Look," I said, "let's forget about this and enjoy our dinner. Maybe talk about the play."

Emily talked like an eloquent magpie while I basked in her exuberance. When the Bananas Foster Flambé arrived I told her about the art auction at the Ritz.

"How do you rate such an invitation, Dad?"

I cleared my throat. "A woman I knew from college invited you and me."

"Oh. A rival?" asked Emily, alert.

"Nah, I met her way before I met your mother."

"I gotta keep my eye on you, Dad. Can't have a handsome dude like you on the loose." Emily leaned forward and beamed. "I'd love to go. It'll help take my mind off Monday's lousy rehearsal anyway."

I briefed Emily on my fortuitous meeting with Rebecca, emphasizing her Catholic background, as we topped off our dinner with Rémy Martin.

* * *

On Monday, I picked up Emily at the Asolo stage door. "Do you want to drive, Emily?" I said cheerfully.

"No thanks," said Emily. She leaned back and looked out her side window as we pulled away from the Asolo.

"You seem preoccupied," I offered.

"Just thinking about rehearsal."

After a few miles on crowded Tamiami, Emily looked over at me and put her hand on my arm. "Dad, what's this woman really like anyway?"

"I hadn't seen her in over twenty years." I concentrated on my driving as a bright red Alfa Romeo cut in front of me. "Damn—so I can't tell you much, because I never communicated with her much."

"Much?"

"Some letters for a few years after she left for Texas to marry a rich oil baron." I felt the edge of anger biting into my good humor. "Way before I met your mother."

I looked over at Emily, gazing straight ahead.

"Does she have children?"

"She tells me none of her own but three by marriage."

"Why?"

"Infertile."

"Oh."

I could feel a prickle of sweat run down my collar. I notched up the air conditioner and became clammy. Emily remained silent as we arrived at the Ritz and I handed the keys to an overdressed valet.

We entered the elevator that took us to the Presidential Suite on the top floor. I looked over at Emily.

"Don't worry Dad, I won't scratch her eyes out." She gave me a stiff grin. "I'm really curious about her."

"I hope you two don't try to cut each other off at the knees."

The attendant who answered the door directed us into a spacious living room overlooking Sarasota Bay.

Rebecca came in from the dining room. "I'm Rebecca Long. Glad to meet you at last. I've heard so much about you."

"And I of you," said Emily primly, gathering emphasis with the final word. "It must be interesting to meet somebody after such a long absence from their life."

"Won't you please sit down?" said Rebecca.

She waved us to a divan. "Can I get you a drink?" Still standing, Rebecca folded her hands together and pointed joined forefingers to a small bar in the corner. "I can have a solid Martini made for you."

"I'd like one," I said.

"A Chardonnay would be okay, I guess," said Emily.

Rebecca turned to a floating waiter to order drinks. "You were wonderful in the play the other night, Emily. May I call you Emily?"

"Please do."

"How long have you been a student at Asolo?"

"This will be my second year."

"I've always admired McMurtry, especially *Lonesome Dove*. My

46

favorite though is *The Last Picture Show*."

"Yes, its focus on a neglected woman is superb," said Emily, without missing a beat.

I caught Rebecca's glance just as Alex entered the room. "Well, who do we have here?"

Rebecca made introductions. Alex dominated the conversation for the next half-hour with stories about his Texas boyhood.

"My Daddy wanted us to be able to take over the reins of the company," said Alex. He handed his glass to a waiter for another Martini. "Now Becky knows as much about the company as I do. Isn't that right, love?"

"I suppose." Rebecca continued to sip on her first Martini. "Why don't we look at some of the auction paintings in the ballroom," suggested Rebecca.

"Good idea," said Alex, as the waiter returned to hand him another Martini.

In the elevator to the ballroom, Alex started an animated conversation with Emily that gave me a chance to talk with Rebecca.

"Your daughter would like to plunge a knife into my heart, Peter."

"She sees you as a rival, just trying to protect her mother."

"Maybe I am." Rebecca turned as Emily came up to us and grabbed me by the elbow.

"Come here, Dad. I want to show you some paintings." She pulled me toward one corner of the room. "She's beautiful." Emily held onto my arm and pretended to look at a watercolor. "Do you still like her?"

"Look Emily, she's an old girlfriend, that's all."

"You're still in her sights if you ask me."

"Have some faith in your old man, will you?"

"Okay, but I'm keeping an eye on you." She grabbed me by the arm and leaned against me a moment as Rebecca came over to us.

"Let me show you some oil paintings, Emily, set in McMurtry's home town," said Rebecca. She pointed to a corridor of paintings and cupped Emily's elbow toward them. Alex asked me whether I'd ever seen an original Colt revolver and whisked me away in the same direction.

Later, when Alex insisted Emily scan Sarasota Bay from their top floor suite, I found myself alone with Rebecca.

"She's smart, talented, and utterly protective of her father."

"And also of her mother."

"You know you might have been the father of my daughter."

"You made a choice."

"You could have told me you loved me and I might have changed my mind about the abortion."

She paused, waiting.

"But you never told me."

"No."

Rebecca turned towards me. Her skin reflected the desolate coloration of the McMurtry paintings that surrounded us. She smiled a slowly-fading smile, her pale blue eyes glistening.

She turned and reached for my hand as we walked down the corridor to the elevator. "I feel like one of McMurtry's abandoned women."

I felt her hand loosen from mine.

Driving back to Emily's apartment, Emily broke the silence. "Rebecca feels to me like one of McMurtry's outcasts."

"You like her don't you?"

"Yeah, sort of."

"She looks a little like you."

"So does Mom."

"I'll be calling your mother tonight."

"You don't owe Rebecca anything."

"I know."

London Bridges

Since early childhood, Geoffrey Harrison III had hated to puke. It was 5 a.m. and he punched the alarm clock. Fingers of sunlight poked through the half-open Venetian blinds. During the night he had startled several times and rushed to the bathroom until the nausea wore off. His father said only sissies threw up.

He returned to the bedroom and sat down on his bed. The bed sagged and settled around him. Maria was turned away, spoon-like. Fortunately, she had always been a sound sleeper. Geoffrey selected his Hickey Freeman suit from the closet. He decided to dress downstairs so he wouldn't disturb her.

The taste of bile crept up again as Geoffrey went over to his armoire, reached into a small compartment, pulled out a snub-nosed Smith and Wesson, and shoved it into his bathrobe pocket. He wobbled into the hallway and paused. A wave of dizziness passed. The revolver bumped his thigh as he steadied himself on the banister and descended to the first floor. He retched in a corridor bathroom, on his knees, hugging the cool porcelain. Last night Maria had made lasagna.

Geoffrey hung over the commode until he felt the euphoric release from nausea. He stood and propped himself against the wall to wait for dizziness to pass before walking into the hallway toward the kitchen. His hand shot out onto the kitchen island table to catch himself from falling. A corner of the table speared his hip. He braced himself on the cool tile surface and closed his eyes until the pain let up. When he opened his eyes he looked down on pictures of the London Bridge embedded in the tile. *Falling down, falling down.* An image of his son Peter flashed into his mind, the boy's wide eyes crumpling at the edges and slowly closing. *Falling down.* Geoffrey caught himself bent and swaying slightly.

He straightened stiffly, turned around to open the sliding glass doors, and stepped out onto the deck that surrounded the oversized pool. The refreshing morning breeze distracted Geoffrey as he stood by the pool.

"You didn't tell me you planned to leave so early," said Maria.

Geoffrey jerked around and faced Maria. "No. I changed my mind." Geoffrey felt a drop of sweat crawl down his neck.

Maria frowned. "What's the matter?"

"Nothing."

She waited. Geoffrey turned back toward the pool. He rocked back and forth on the balls of his feet.

"Something's bugging you. What is it?"

He shrugged. "Nothing."

"Goddammit tell me what it is Geoffrey." She spoke so quickly that it all sounded like a single word, then his name.

Geoffrey sighed. "Last night, when we were discussing the turnpike bridge project—" Geoffrey could taste the bile in his throat. "I didn't come clean on our estimates. They were way under cost."

"Geoffrey, why not?"

"I don't know. Father would have been livid. The underestimate may bankrupt Harrison and Byrd."

"But you've got to tell him," said Maria.

He turned, shifting his bathrobe so that the revolver's bulge couldn't be seen. "Why? Father doesn't believe anything I say anyway."

Maria's olive skin glowed in the dawn light. She sniffed the air. "Are you alright? Are you feeling sick again?"

"Those monthly family corporate meetings like the one last night make a wreck out of me." No sense denying it. Maria always saw through him.

Maria shook loose her glossy black hair and rubbed her hand across the back of his neck. The rubbing caused a stir in his groin, rare nowadays. They both gazed at the dawning August sun that burned through the overcast like a giant spying eye.

"Maybe I ought to quit," said Geoffrey. "Get out from under his thumb."

Maria gave him a sharp look. "Why Geoffrey? Why not stick it out? He's got to give in sometime."

Maria hesitated. Geoffrey could fill in the blank. His father would eventually die, maybe soon. He already was on his third bypass repair, and stents were no longer effective.

"Geoffrey, you're the brains in your father's business, especially when it comes to building bridges."

Geoffrey squinted into the sun to hide a welling of tears. "You and my father are like two peas in a pod. He adores you. Me, he gives all the responsibility, while he makes all the decisions." Geoffrey wasn't able to say he couldn't stand up to his father like she could.

She opened her mouth to tell him again to stand up to his father, but he cut her off.

"I've got to get going. Father wants me in the office early to follow up on last night's talk." Geoffrey sighed. "I love you Maria. You're the best thing that ever happened to me."

He held her for a long moment. "Give Peter a hug for me when he wakes up. Tell him I love him."

When he let go she looked at him closely and cocked her head. "He knows. He loves you too."

"I've got to run," said Geoffrey.

After a shower and talc to blot out a lingering odor, Geoffrey dressed and placed the Smith and Wesson in his briefcase. The spirited maroon BMW he chose from the three-car garage was Maria's favorite and often his superstitious choice. He doubted the choice would change his mind today. In fact it might make him more determined.

Maria was leaning on one of the columns near the front door as he pulled out of the garage. He lowered the window. "I—I love you."

"Yeah. Me too," said Maria, still puzzled. "Call me from the office later."

"Sure."

When he was out of her sight he gave way to tears. His father had once beat him with a belt for running and crying to his mother. *You're a sissy, a crybaby, a mommy's boy! You've got to learn to stand up for yourself!* The belt had rained down on his eight year-old bottom until his mother threatened to call the police. Her intervention was rare, and it would cost her later.

The route between Geoffrey's York home and his office in Harrisburg was undergoing its yearly summer reconstruction, and the traffic was formidable as usual. The habitual resignation tried to creep in but could not find any purchase today. Today, Geoffrey planned to drive only part way and register at a Sheraton.

Geoffrey tightened his grip on the steering wheel when he spotted the construction barriers leading to Harrisburg. He sucked in air with rapid shallow breaths as vehicles slowed. Traffic compacted into a single lane, a car a few feet ahead and a car a few feet behind, jammed front-to-back while squeezed side-to-side by the concrete barriers. *Real men don't let anyone push them around. How are you ever going to grow up, acting like that?* The urge to stop and bolt out the door froze in his mind. But where would he go?

A horn blared behind him. The silver Lexus in front had moved several yards ahead and Geoffrey accelerated quickly, almost crashing into it. *Get a grip! Get a grip!* His mantra burned into his mind. His movements seemed distant to him, as though not his own. He felt like he was being manipulated by a puppeteer.

He remembered his psychiatrist had peered over his half-glasses and told him: *"What do you want to do Geoffrey? You are living a 'strings attached' life. It's time to decide what you want to do."*

He tried to let his mind wander. *Falling down. Falling down.* He loosened his grip on the steering wheel. *Build it up with iron bars. Iron bars.* A plan settled heavily in his mind, as if the plan had been holding itself up above his mind for a long time. *Iron bars will bend and break.* The thought of the revolver in his briefcase tugged at him. Traffic began to progress smoothly. He turned onto the exit ramp leading to the hotel, still operating like an automaton, and parked in the lot. Geoffrey sat back just as his cell phone jarred him to attention. He wiped his sweaty hands with a handkerchief and punched the vibrating phone to life.

"Hello. Geoffrey here."

"Geoffrey. Is that you? I've been trying to reach you all morning."

"Maria. Yes, it's me."

"Your father is dead. His heart..." Maria gasped. "Geoffrey, I'm so sorry."

Yes. So am I. Geoffrey could feel his eyes soften with tears. He steeled himself against their flow, as he had been taught to do.

"Geoffrey! Are you there? Are you at the office?"

"No. Not yet."

"Where are you?"

"Traffic is jammed pretty badly through the construction sites today. I'm stuck in the middle of it." Geoffrey's voice echoed through his head.

"Your father was taken to Polyclinic Hospital but he died on arrival," said Maria. "We'll need to make funeral arrangements. Call the others. I don't know what to do."

Geoffrey didn't answer. "Geoffrey?"

"I better get to the office."

"Why don't you come home and we'll do what has to be done together."

"No. They'll need me at the office—things pending. I'll inform them about Father and call you later." Geoffrey hesitated. "I love you."

"And I love you."

Geoffrey grabbed his briefcase from the seat, opened the car door, and walked to the hotel entrance. Inside, he hurried past a pungent array of roses that lined the foyer and bracketed the registration desk. He stared at the pretty clerk impatiently tapping her pencil. Her blue-black hair was done in small curls much like Maria's. He blinked himself to attention and signed his name as the Maria look-alike flashed a tolerant smile.

Geoffrey slid the plastic key into the lock. In the room, he closed the fresh smelling drapes and sat down on the twin bed. He reached behind him to pull the briefcase onto his lap, opened it, picked up the Smith and Wesson with its brimming cylinder of bullets, and shoved the briefcase onto the floor. He gazed at the metallic blue hardness that lay in his limp hand.

How do you go about killing yourself when you really want to kill your father? His psychiatrist had once told him there was a first time for everything.

Geoffrey began to laugh. *A first time for everything!* He couldn't stop laughing. His laughter became hysterical. Yes, he was now the owner of a company driven into bankruptcy by his father, a tyrant who nobody but his wife had dared to confront. He gripped harder on the pistol. He felt more in control but numb, no love, no hate for his father. His father was gone, and Geoffrey was the only one he had to hate now.

The ring of his cell phone squelched the laughter that had brought tears to his eyes.

"Geoffrey here."

There was a pause. "Is this you, Geoffrey?"

"Yes, Maria."

My fair lady.

"You sound funny, Geoffrey. Are you okay? They've called from the office, wondering what happened to you. I didn't tell them about your father, like you said."

Geoffrey didn't recognize his own voice either, which said, briskly, "Maria, I'll take care of the office. I want you to call Frohley's, the undertaker the family uses, and make arrangements. Inform the kids, the lawyer, the accountant. Chrysanthemums, I've always liked those. Get those. After that, have a bath and make something for dinner."

Maria hesitated. "All right Geoffrey."

When Geoffrey called the office, he recognized the voice of his father's longtime secretary.

"Byrd and Harrison."

"Ms. Adams, my father has just passed away."

There was silence before a weakened voice responded. "Yes?"

"I've been held up in traffic. Do not do anything until I arrive to make some decisions."

"But...there are things pending..."

Ms. Adams' voice trailed off as Geoffrey interrupted. "Do I make myself clear, Ms. Adams?" Geoffrey waited out the silence until she responded.

"Yes sir. You do, sir." The second "sir" was punctuated by an emphatic gap.

After Geoffrey ended his call, he glanced at the stubby revolver that he had set on the bed. He picked up the briefcase from the floor, placed the weapon back into it, and snapped it shut.

Geoffrey hurried out the door to his car. The bridge into Harrisburg glistened in the distance.

Meth

The throbbing pain in Deena's ankle crept upward, cramping her leg. Meth had given her the nerve to jump from the second-story window. She'd slammed into the ground, pain rushing to her head like a sledgehammer. The wind was knocked out of her and she fought against passing out. She couldn't walk at first.

Shit, I must have busted my leg! She realized later that she hadn't, otherwise walking the mile or so from Jordan Home would have been impossible.

Deena knew the short-handed staff couldn't keep track of everything. Besides, the staff probably thought the threat of a thunderstorm would give the kids second thoughts about running away. Jamie, a young counselor, almost messed up her plan when he caught her near the window as she estimated the jump she had to make. Deena told him she sometimes sleepwalks. He couldn't think his way out of a paper bag.

She wanted to sit down and rest awhile. *No way!* Waiting for the pain to wear off would only increase her chances of being caught and dragged back to Jordan Home. She walked until the pain demanded she stop.

Despite telling herself not to, Deena started to cry—softly at first, until sobbing took over. She sat propped against a tree that spread its leaves part-way over the country road, no plan in mind.

Maybe she should return, take restriction, and work her way back into favor with the staff. She would have to face the creepy Assistant Director who was extra friendly to Deena. His beard pointed down over his chin and his eyes bored into her. He often stared at her when he thought she wasn't looking. She dodged his attempts to have a "friendly chat" in his office about the "good-for-a-sixteen-year-old" foster homes.

Deena wiped away the last of her tears. She was determined to connect with Kayla in Pittsburgh. Kayla had been her friend in several foster homes and kept in touch with her through monthly phone calls. Kayla taught Deena how to drive and cross ignition wires. Last year, a joyride with Kayla led to placement in the same detention center.

"You could pass for someone ten years older," Kayla once told Deena. That remark made their relationship solid. She didn't know whether Kayla was more like an older sister or a mother. How would she know? Deena never had a sister and her mother died when she was a toddler.

Deena turned to face the tree and, hand over hand, pulled herself upward off the ground. That's when she saw the same pickup truck that had passed her a mile back. She wondered why it had returned.

The pickup's headlights glared through the darkness, weaving back and forth across the center line, searching for something. As Deena leaned against the tree, the vehicle headed towards her and pulled off the road nearby. She turned to run. Her leg gave way and she fell, grabbing a tree for support. She decided to stand her ground, take her chances. Besides, she was hobbled.

A lone driver peered out of the cab window, a baseball cap tilted on the back of his head. "Can I give you a lift?" The friendly voice sounded young. "I'll be turning around, headed back in the same direction you're going."

Deena hesitated, yet she was eager to get the hell out of there and on to Pittsburgh. It was time to move on.

"Sure can." She rose from her propped stance. "I'm a little lame."

"You need help?" he asked.

"No. Sprained my ankle a while back. I'll be okay."

Deena limped towards the passenger door, which opened up for her. She slid into the passenger seat, unable to avoid a wince.

"How far ya going?" he asked.

"Going to a town near Pittsburgh. How far are you going?"

"Oh, not quite that far." He steered the pickup onto the road and turned it around. "You're a long way from Pittsburgh. Why Pittsburgh?"

"Relatives there." A lie. An aunt she hardly knew lived in Philadelphia, but she had no relatives in Pittsburgh.

"You from around here?" Deena asked.

"Yep. Not far from here. Lived around here most of my life. What's your name?"

"Deena. What's yours?"

"Tanner." He glanced at her, raised one eyebrow, and rested his palms on the steering wheel. His relaxed manner bugged her. *Too relaxed.*

Several miles had passed, neither of them saying much, when Tanner jerked forward. He peered out the windshield at a kaleidoscope of flashing lights reflected in the cloudy sky ahead.

Tanner slowed down, snapped on the radio, and fished through several stations until he got local news. He leaned forward to catch a report that a middle-aged man had been shot to death a few hours ago.

Tanner leaned back and gripped hard on the steering wheel. He pulled alongside the road, sighed, sat back, and turned to look over at Deena.

"Bet you didn't expect this?" said Tanner, his smile flat, like a billboard.

Deena turned away to open the door, but Tanner clicked it locked from the driver's side. She turned back to face him, not knowing what to expect.

"Do ya know how to drive?"

"Yeah," came the truth. She was too freaking scared to think up a lie.

"Have a driver's license?"

Deena nodded. She had taken a driver's license from the Honda Civic she and Kayla had stolen a year ago. She kept the license because the likeness was striking and she thought, who knows, someday it might come in handy.

Tanner leaned towards her, one knee almost touching hers while his thin arm lay along the top of the seat behind her.

"You may have to drive," he said, as he faced her, his head cocked to one side.

She stared at his large eyes set in a face too small for them. He looked like a poster child for a leukemia ad. His boozy breath had thickened in the closed cab.

"Whadda'ya staring at?"

"Nothing. Just know you're in some kind of trouble."

"How'd you figure that out?" said Tanner, his voice sarcastic.

"What kind of trouble?"

"Never mind that. You're going to get me through this roadblock." Tanner yanked his baseball cap tight over his head. He reached across Deena and opened the glove compartment. He pulled out a large handgun.

Deena pressed her back against the passenger door. "Didn't you ever try to get some help from somewhere for whatever is going on?" Deena's voice cracked with anxiety.

His lopsided grin encouraged her to go on. "Look, I know you've suffered something I don't understand. I've suffered too. You don't trust anybody but yourself. Or maybe somebody in the same situation. Me, I'm a runaway from Jordan Home."

"Yep, I figured as much. But you're my ticket out of here now."

She reached for her shoulder bag. Tanner raised the oversized pistol towards her.

"No funny stuff."

"No. I just wanted to get something out of my bag that might help." Tanner lowered the pistol. "Okay, go ahead."

She opened her bag and pulled out a Kleenex. Three pills were folded in it.

"This might help you get through to wherever you're going. It's meth, some call it ice. Helps steady your nerves."

"Never tried anything beyond weed and booze." Tanner frowned.

"I only take this when I really need it. Helped me a while ago. Try it."

Tanner reached under the seat and pulled out a half-empty fifth of Old Grandad. He picked out one of the strange pills and rolled it suspiciously in the palm of his hand before washing it down with the whiskey.

After a few minutes Tanner shrugged his shoulders like he expected an immediate effect.

"It doesn't work right away. It'll make you dizzy at first. That'll wear off fast. Then you'll feel good, be alert, and get a plan in your head. It'll be a plan for now, and it'll open you up for later, make you see what's ahead of you in life."

They waited quietly for a few more minutes. Deena had taken the same pill hours ago to give her the guts to jump from the second story window. She had been tempted to take another. She knew the odd-shaped pill had many effects. Deena counted on it now to make Tanner talkative and open to suggestion. A gamble.

Several minutes later Tanner began talking more. He talked about beatings by his stepfather, Hiram. He pulled up his jacket sleeve to reveal skin peppered with old cigarette burns put there by Hiram.

"The son of a bitch was always saying he'd shoot me in the head with his .457 Magnum. When he took his daytime nap, my mom and I never knew whether he would wake up like a wild man—waving it all over the place, threatening us with it, claiming we kept him awake."

Tanner's speech became hurried, uninterruptible. He paused and turned towards Deena. He shook his head, slumped back in the driver's seat, and curled his thin body under the steering wheel. "I shot my old

60

man." Tanner's spiritless eyes sprung into focus and locked onto Deena. "Not my real father, my stepfather."

Deena could see frenzied beads of sweat on Tanner's forehead. His vaporizing breath and sweat filled the closed cab air with dizzying alcoholic fumes.

"Never mind the gory details." His voice trailed off and sounded more like a child's whine. Tanner grabbed the steering wheel to pull himself up and stared out the windshield. "Wasn't going to let Hiram beat up on my mom one more time."

Tanner turned towards Deena again. "The bastard came home, drunker than usual, went right after my mom." Tanner paused to look past Deena, his eyes two blank discs.

"I grabbed the Magnum he always kept under his pillow." For the moment Tanner sounded more like an in-charge adult. "Told him to back off. He didn't. So I shot him. End of story."

Deena had difficulty understanding his rush of words. "Couldn't you've called the police?"

"You kidding! They'd just say he has the right to be head of his family, command respect."

Tanner looked out the windshield again. Deena could see flashing multicolored lights reflected in the corner of his eye. He turned back towards Deena.

"And my mother, ya oughta hear her. Always believed it wouldn't happen again. How many times did it have to happen to convince her he wouldn't change? The police, they're useless!"

"You could give yourself up, tell them your stepfather threatened to kill you with his gun."

"Yeah, sure. That's like when I begged for my dog."

"Begged for your dog?"

"I was five years old and had a puppy. Named him Toby. I couldn't get him house-trained so Hiram made me go into the woods with him to watch him shoot Toby. Told me if I didn't stop begging not to shoot Toby he'd shoot me!"

Tears dribbled down Tanner's face. He turned again to Deena and leaned towards her, stone-faced. He gripped hard on the Magnum and raised it towards her, his eyes packed with menace. "Yeah, I've got a plan all right. And you're part of it," said Tanner, the quietness of his words scary.

"You're going to drive and say all the right things. You hear me?" Tanner shoved the Magnum closer to Deena. "They'll be less suspicious of a woman."

This is no time to interrupt him. Deena merely nodded. Things had become more screwed up.

He pushed Deena out the passenger side, followed her around to the driver's side, and waved her into the cab with the Magnum. He locked the doors and returned to the passenger side, unlocked it, and slid in beside her. He took another nervous look out the windshield.

"You know you could plead self-defense," Deena said under her breath.

Tanner whirled around and pointed the Magnum towards Deena, close to her head. Blood throbbed through her neck in rhythm with Tanner's shaking gun hand. He inched back the Magnum.

"Just drive, will ya? You told me I'd find a plan. So this is it."

She drove the pickup onto the road and joined the line of vehicles that idled up to the flashing checkpoint. A trooper approached them, his Smokey-the-Bear hat squared on his head. Deena felt the urge to pee her pants.

"Where you headed?" asked the trooper, one hand on the door sill as he peered into the cab, eye-level with both Deena and Tanner. Deena looked slightly past the trooper's face and concentrated on his right ear to keep herself calm.

"Pittsburgh, officer," said Deena, her voice squeaky.

Tanner handed the trooper the registration and his license. The

62

trooper looked at it briefly and handed it back across Deena.

"Your license, young lady?"

With her sweaty hands, Deena fumbled for the license in her shoulder bag. The trooper took it. He looked at Deena for a long moment and then back at the plastic-coated license before he handed it back.

"Drive careful." The trooper waved them on.

A few miles later Tanner told Deena to pull over and exchange seats. Just as he pulled away, screeching sirens ripped the air. They looked behind at an expanding criss-cross of lights.

"Tanner, give yourself up. Things will work out, you'll see," she begged.

Tanner gave Deena an odd smile and swerved into a dirt road. He barreled the pickup several hundred yards down the rut-filled road. He looked back at the whirling lights. When he looked forward again it was too late to avoid a huge oak tree. The pickup bounced off the tree, into a tank-trap-sized ditch, and rolled. When it righted itself it was stuck.

Tanner bolted out the door and headed towards the nearby woods. There was an order to halt. Shots rang out and Tanner fell.

Deena stumbled from the pickup. She reached into her shoulder bag for the meth and ditched it into the deep grass where she knelt. A chunky-looking trooper emerged from the hodgepodge of glimmering vehicles and jogged towards her. When he reached her he jerked her onto her feet. Deena knew the drill and like a well-trained dog put her hands behind her to be cuffed.

"You'll need to come with me." The trooper pulled her by the elbow past a boxy ambulance that had beeped its way through the disarray of cruisers. Deena saw Tanner about to be lifted into the ambulance. She was close enough to see the neat hole in the front of his stained leather jacket. Deena heard a faint voice. "Toby."

Second Chance

The Springville fire alarm blasted so loud I fell off the fence and tore my pants. The siren's screech made my skin tingle so much I almost forgot about how mad Mom would be for ripping my pants. And for pulling the fire alarm.

The big kids hustled out the high school door. The wind blew leaves around them and they hugged themselves to keep warm.

"Line up over here," a teacher yelled.

When the long ladder fire engine drove up, I ran to it. I ducked under the ladder sticking out the back to get a good look. A fireman wearing a shiny yellow raincoat spotted me. "Get out of there, kid!"

Rolly, the fire chief, dashed into the school. Everybody called him Rolly because he was mostly bald and he looked like a rolling donut when he walked down the street. When he came out of the school, I spotted him looking straight at me. He wrinkled his nose as though he got a whiff of skunk cabbage. I dodged around a couple of firemen laying down hoses and setting up fire ladders. I knew I'd landed in big trouble when Rolly grabbed me and swung me around. "What are you doing in this schoolyard!"

I was eleven and not that big so there was no way he'd believe I was one of the high-schoolers.

"My school lets out earlier than the high school."

A fireman in black knee boots and a red pointed fire hat leaned a ladder against the school building. Rolly shouted at him. "We've got a false alarm here, Tim. Put the ladder back!"

I started to sneak away, but Rolly saw me and shook his head. "Oh no you don't," he said, leading me to one of the schoolyard benches. "Sit!" He jerked his finger downward and stood over me. He glared at me until I sat.

Rolly sat down next to me and folded his thick arms, resting them on his belly like a shelf. "Okay, let's have the truth. Why are you in this schoolyard?"

"Because I wanted to play dodgeball with the big kids. I always win at dodgeball with kids my age."

Rolly sighed. "But you know you're not supposed to be monkeying around here. Right?"

"Yes, sir. Mom says not to play with the bigger kids because I fall down a lot and get poison blood."

"Poison blood?"

"Uh-huh. I have to put some hot stuff on it to get out the poison when I get cut. My parents get mad about it because that stuff—it looks like clay and smells like burnt toast—costs a lot of money."

A thought struck me and I jumped up from the bench. Rolly pushed me back. "No you don't."

"If that stuff costs a lot of money, why did Dad give peanut butter sandwiches to the hoboes who knocked at our back door? That costs money too."

Rolly put both hands on his knees. "You're an odd one, aren't you?"

"Dad says most of the hoboes living under the trestle are good people who want to get back to their families. That's why I walk to the trestle to listen to their stories."

"Your parents let you go to the trestle to talk with the hoboes?"

"No, I have to sneak out."

Rolly looked at me funny.

65

"After my little brother fell through the ice, Dad stopped making peanut butter sandwiches for the hoboes." I stared at my sneakers, waiting for Rolly to change the subject like Mom and Dad always did whenever I talked about Eddy's drowning, but Rolly just sat there, listening. "Dad and Eddy were close because Eddy couldn't catch his breath. Sometimes Eddy stayed up most of the night to get his breathing to come back."

Rolly leaned forward, both hands still on his knees. "How did it happen?" He spoke real soft like Grandma does when she talks about Eddy, so I knew he wanted to hear more about it.

"Eddy skated over to the thin ice where Dad told him not to skate."

"Wasn't anybody there to stop him?"

"Dad can skate lickety-split but didn't reach Eddy in time. A doctor skating on the creek tried to get his breathing started. It didn't work."

"I'm sorry about your brother."

Suddenly I felt like crying. "They still yell about it all the time. Mom yells at Dad. Dad yells at Mom. Eddy this. Eddy that. What if you…No, what if you…"

I looked down at my sneakers brushing back and forth on the ground. "I kind of think it's my fault too and wish I'd warned Eddy more about the thin ice. When I go to the trestle the hoboes tell me about all the bad things they've done. They're sorry too."

The big kids watched me with Rolly as the firemen wound the hoses piled up on the grass.

"Hey Jake, wind up that hose tighter will you?" yelled Rolly. He turned back to me. "Do you miss your brother?"

"I hid his favorite baseball card. Joe DiMaggio. Eddy went around for days thinking it got mashed up in the wash." I wiped my nose on the back of my hand. "After he fell through the ice, we collected all his stuff and put it in his room. Joe DiMaggio too. But I don't like to go past Eddy's room. When they dragged him out of the water he looked like one of those plastic dolls. Maybe they pulled out a different boy."

"The hoboes say if you've been missing long enough you may want to return to an earlier life and start over. Do you believe that? I have this feeling that he hasn't stayed buried and he's living with us in his room. That one day he may just pop out."

Rolly put his hand on my shoulder. "Your brother had a Christian burial. I remember seeing it in the paper. He's not going to pop out if he's been buried."

"It would be like a second chance," I continued. "If Eddy came back he'd be more careful, Mom and Dad would watch him better, and he could have a brother who just doesn't stand there and watch him drown."

I rubbed my hands together. They felt sore from holding onto the bench so hard and I was feeling a little dizzy.

"It sounds like you want a second chance yourself," said Rolly.

Rolly looked around. The fire engines were gone. The big kids were back in their school. The wind had died down.

"It was bad to have fire engines come here when they didn't have to," said Rolly. "You ready to tell me the truth?"

But the way he looked at me, I could tell he already knew.

"I pulled the fire alarm."

Rolly's expression didn't change. "There could have been another fire while the fire engines were here and somebody's house could have burned down."

"I'm sorry." I was trying not to cry.

"Why would you do such a fool thing?"

"I saw Eddy running out of the schoolyard."

"You saw a boy who you *thought* looked like your brother?" Rolly peeked over the top of his glasses.

"Yeah. He wore the New York Yankees baseball shirt Dad gave Eddy for his birthday."

Rolly took off his glasses and held them in his hand.

"I shouted at him that it was me and that I'd be right there, but he ran away faster."

Rolly pulled back his two chins.

"He got glassy looking and I could almost see through him. Then he disappeared. Just disappeared!"

"But why pull the alarm?"

"I wanted Eddy to come back. I had to make him hear me. When I broke the glass it sounded like cracking ice."

Rolly put his fire hat back on and stood. "Let's go," he said. "You can ride home in my truck."

"Aren't you going to arrest me or something?" I asked.

"Nah," Rolly said, putting his hat on my head. "Everyone deserves a second chance."

Resurrection

Alicia left her psychiatrist's nineteenth-floor office and hurried to the elevator. She stood near the door during the interminable descent. Sweat trickled down her forehead. On the ground floor she rushed to a hallway bench and leaned back against the marble wall, letting its icy coolness curb her anxiety.

Her husband Peter arrived to take her home. She stood and walked towards him, unsteady, but determined to will away her lightheadedness.

"Hello Alicia," said Peter. "How did it go today?"

"Okay, I guess." She wondered how other patients talked about the hours with their psychiatrist. Besides, she felt Peter wished she'd snap out of it.

She walked with Peter toward the parking lot, trying to match his loping gait. "Peter, slow down!" Even though his career with the Philadelphia 76ers ended with a shattered knee, Alicia had to strain to keep up with his long, uneven strides.

"Sorry Alicia," murmured Peter, as they continued at a slower pace to the parking lot.

Alicia glanced up at Peter's fair-skinned face. The light spray of freckles made him seem boyish, young for his age.

As Peter drove she saw a school bus release a squadron of early teens, knapsacks bulging with books. Why are children so helplessly weighted down, she wondered.

"Alicia," said Peter, breaking through her reverie, "really, how did it go today?" Peter slammed on the brakes for the school bus as it discharged another load of students. "Did he encourage you to drive again?"

"Of course," she lied.

Peter glanced at Alicia as she stared straight ahead. Neither of them spoke for the rest of the trip home.

After Peter returned to his office, Alicia saw the new neighbor's daughter playing with a kitten in their backyard. She fought down revulsion and focused on the child, noticing her smooth hair and snub nose in a face too small for her oversized eyes. Alicia guessed she was a pre-teen until she moved closer to see budding breasts pressing through a close-fitting blouse.

"What's your name?" asked Alicia.

The girl shrank back, her large eyes stretched even wider as she scooped up the kitten and headed toward her backdoor.

"Wait! I'm not going to hurt you," said Alicia.

The girl stopped after a few steps and turned around. "I'm not supposed to tell you," said the girl, her voice barely audible.

"But I live next door," said Alicia.

"It's Melissa," said the girl, hesitant, still poised to retreat.

"That's a nice name. My name is Alicia." Alicia took a slow, small step forward. Melissa remained still.

"How old are you?" asked Alicia.

"Twelve." She ducked her eyes and hugged the kitten.

Alicia took a deep breath. "Is that your kitten?"

"Yep. I just got her yesterday. I named her Tabby," said Melissa. Alicia felt dizzy.

"That's a nice name, too. I had a kitten like that once. Looked something like your calico there." The words came out in a rush of air, and Alicia only now realized she had been holding it in.

"You just moved in here?"

"Uh-huh."

"Do you have any sisters or brothers?"

"Nope. I'm the only one."

"Melissa! Where are you?" someone yelled from the neighbor's backdoor.

"That's my mother. I gotta go."

Melissa's mother hurried toward them. "Melissa, I told you to get in here for dinner a half-hour ago."

"I'm Alicia Hammond, your new next-door neighbor," said Alicia, extending her hand. Melissa's mother looked her up and down but did not extend hers, instead brushing away wisps of brown hair and frowning at her daughter.

Melissa tightened her grip on the kitten as she looked up at her mother. Alicia forced herself to unclench her shoulders.

"Get in the house," ordered the mother, stabbing her finger toward their backdoor. "Your dinner's getting cold."

Melissa scurried toward the backdoor and wordlessly entered with Tabby clutched in her arms. The woman turned to Alicia.

"I'm Inez Smith." Her eyes darted past Alicia as though searching for something only she could see.

"It's nice to meet you. I'm sure we'll see more of each other," said Alicia. An awkward silence followed.

"Let me know if she bothers you," said Inez, turning to begin a brisk walk toward her back door.

That night, Alicia startled awake and bolted upright, perspiring. She often had dreams of being alone and unable to move. That wasn't it. She heard voices coming from next door.

Moonlight shone through filmy curtains wafting in the nighttime breeze. There it was again—a soft moan only a child could make coming from the new neighbor's house. She heard a scraping noise, maybe a screen door banging closed, followed by more voices, sometimes high-pitched, a woman's voice, then a tinkling sound, perhaps shattering glass.

Alicia looked over at Peter, doggedly asleep, his long body curved spoon-like on the far side of the bed. She heard a door slam from the house next door, maybe the garage door. Was her mind playing tricks on her again, thinking about something so hard that it seemed true?

She pulled her pillow up onto the headboard and leaned back, listening hard, but heard nothing more.

"I met our new neighbors," Alicia told her psychiatrist, Doctor Ross, at her next session.

"And?"

"They have an only child, a twelve-year-old daughter. I met her in the backyard. She seemed attached to her kitten."

"That's interesting."

"She looked frightened when her mother came out of the house to get her for dinner."

"Why do you say that?"

"I've been around kids long enough to know when they're feeling overwhelmed." Alicia's anger surprised her.

"Yes, I know you have, Alicia."

Alicia gripped hard on the arms of the high-backed Danish chair. She reached into her pocketbook for a tissue and dabbed away tears. She moved the pocketbook behind her chair.

"You alright, Alicia?"

"I'm sorry. The odor of my new pocketbook made me feel dizzy."

"Dizzy?"

"My thoughts are piling up again." She nodded toward a picture of a stark-white seagull hovering over a rotting lifeboat stuck in the sand. "Stuck like that." She turned back to Doctor Ross peering over his half-glasses. "Where did you say you got that picture, doctor?"

"At an art store in Atlantic City. Why do you ask?"

"Reminds me of the Resurrection."

"Yes?"

"A new beginning."

Alicia's mind went blank and she began to perspire. She felt a panicky urge to leave the room.

"What are you thinking?" asked Doctor Ross.

"I've been more anxious. Like I'm waiting for something to happen," said Alicia.

"Like what?" asked Doctor Ross.

"Last night, the neighbors...I think they were fighting." Alicia held her breath, forced herself to breathe.

"Fighting?"

"I thought for a moment I heard them fighting, briefly. But...Melissa..."

"You thought you heard Melissa?"

"Maybe," said Alicia. She felt a rush of anxiety. "It reminds me of an experience with a boy who used to live down the street from me."

"In what way?"

Alicia took a deep breath and fought down the urge to vomit. "Because one day this boy, Tommy, saw me playing with my kitten. One just like Melissa's. Snatched it away from me. Ran down the street with it to his garage."

"Yes?"

"He poured kerosene over it. Threatened to set it on fire."

"Did you try to get help?"

"His parents pulled in the driveway. When I told them what Tommy had threatened to do, Tommy told them I was going to use the kerosene as a cleanser. And they believed him! When I told my parents they didn't believe me either. They said Tommy Turner would never do such a thing. Bullshit!"

"What happened next?"

"My kitten ran away. Never saw her again."

But it was dead, she knew. She wasn't sure why she couldn't say it out loud. It wasn't her fault. It was Tommy's. Anyone would have done what she did.

Alicia slept lightly the next few nights, waiting for something to happen. In the middle of the week it did. She heard a crash next door followed by the voices of Inez and a man arguing. Doors slammed and noises came from the direction of the neighbor's garage.

Alicia looked at Peter. He was asleep. She slipped out of bed, threw on a robe, and went to the backdoor. She waited for silence before she made her next move. When passing clouds darkened a full moon, she ran toward the Smith's garage window. She fought back labored breathing and listened until the only sound she heard was the sing-song of cicadas. She fumbled for her flashlight and swept the beam across a garage floor scattered with debris like a child's playpen.

A movement in the corner of the garage caught her eye. She moved her light and a cat, bigger than Tabby, cast a long shadow across the garage. It moved suddenly and Alicia lost it. She felt frozen to the ground. Her head pounded, and she felt a drop of sweat jumping from her chin as if in slow motion. Another movement. This time, she fixed the light on a huddled figure, head down on folded arms. The head popped up. Melissa!

Melissa shrieked and bolted to the side door of the garage. Alicia ran to the door to catch her as she ran out. When she put her hand under Melissa's chin to turn up her face, she brushed across a pulpy welt.

"Melissa. It's all right. It's me. Alicia."

Melissa pulled back and pounded Alicia with her fists. "Let me go! Let me go! You're not my mother!" Alicia fell back, letting her go. Melissa ran to her back door, banged it open and disappeared inside. A light flashed on. Alicia pushed back her disheveled hair and wiped away clammy sweat from her face. She stood near the garage and listened, but heard nothing except excited cicadas. The light in the house flicked off. Alicia went to a window and looked into the living room. There was very little furniture, and almost no decorations. No porcelain lamps or candy trays. Several family pictures hung high on the wall, too high to look at without standing on something. She turned and saw another cat, even bigger than the last. It stared at her with emotionless eyes. She meant it no harm, but it didn't believe her. She yelped and backed away, pulling her housecoat close around her.

Alicia's next session with Doctor Ross began with tears. "I felt helpless that I couldn't do something!"

"Did you tell Peter or call the police?"

"Peter could sleep through a train wreck. Besides, he tells me I imagine too much. I felt helpless, just like I did with my parents."

Alicia sprang from her chair and walked to Doctor Ross's desk. She pounded on the desk with a tear-soaked tissue wadded in her fist. "Nobody believed me! Dammit!"

Alicia stood with her back to Doctor Ross until her crying stopped. She looked at the picture of the rotting, stuck lifeboat before turning around. "I've told you over and over again!"

"Alicia, you've told me bits and pieces."

"He tied me up! He gagged me! He tore my clothes off! Don't you believe me?"

"Of course I do. Please sit down."

Alicia could feel the flush of anger on her face replaced by a childish pout that she hated. "You're like my mother. She always said I imagined too much."

"Imagined what?"

"I've told you. He threatened to set my kitten on fire. Doused it with kerosene!"

"That's why you react to strong odors?"

"He damned near burned my kitten to death for Christ's sake and you talk about odors!" Alicia pounded on the arm of her chair. "She always said Tommy Turner couldn't do anything like that, so why would she believe I was raped by Tommy?"

"How old were you?" Doctor Ross looked at Alicia, his eyes steady.

"Twelve."

"Tommy maybe fourteen?" Doctor Ross placed an elbow on the arm of his chair, a forefinger tucked in the cleft of his chin, watchful.

"I guess."

"Did you like Tommy?"

"What, that damned monster!" Alicia jerked upright. "You're pissing me off!"

Alicia looked away for a moment. She couldn't look at Doctor Ross. Her hands shook with the urge to reach out and tear out his eyeballs. When she turned back, she noticed that his lips quivered. Her eyes softened. "I just don't think you know how frustrating it is not to feel believed.

"I believe you."

She felt a warm flush creep into her face. She looked over past Doctor Ross and glanced at the picture of the lifeboat and its hovering seagull. She wondered whether he would be okay with her addressing him by his first name. After all, they'd been in the same room for weekly sessions for the past year. She saw him less like a father figure, more like an equal.

"Okay." Alicia folded her arms like a stubborn teenager. "He lived nearby. He hung around a lot where my school bus let me off. It was the old come-on. He had something to show me. He had something to show me all right."

"What?"

"I can't remember."

"You were interested even though he nearly killed your kitten?"

"That was later." Alicia leaned forward, tense. "Anyway, he was sort of different, charming, I guess."

"So, you were interested in him."

"Curious."

"Just curious?"

"So maybe I had the hots for him." She felt a fresh burst of redness on her cheeks.

"And your mother?"

"It's like she couldn't believe he was bad."

"How did he lure you, Alicia?"

Doctor Ross's calmness irritated her. "All right. I remember," groaned Alicia. "He knew I liked Michael Jackson." She looked away and began to talk under her breath. "He said he'd meet me at my school bus stop and take me to his house to listen to some new Jackson recordings."

"I can't hear you, Alicia."

Alicia jerked around to face Doctor Ross who braced back against his chair. "Can you hear me now?"

"Fine."

"We listened to Jackson recordings. No question about that. But then he had some rope tricks he wanted to show me in his bedroom. Yeah, he showed me all right. He tied me up to his goddamn bedpost!" Alicia jumped up from her chair and paced.

"Sit down, Alicia. I can sense you feel mad at yourself for being so gullible. Remember though, you were only twelve." Doctor Ross leaned towards her.

She sat down, grabbed a tissue, and yanked it so hard that the box ricocheted against Doctor Ross's desk. "I thought he was being cute at first—I was incredibly naïve! He pulled off my skirt, yanked off my blouse, then ripped off my panties."

"So you yelled for help?"

"Yes! But he gagged me. I didn't know how to struggle against him. Today I'd kick a guy in the balls! I didn't feel him enter me, just the stickiness of something dribbling down my legs. It was all over fast." Anger squeezed at Melissa's throat, her breathing uneven. "It was the fucking helplessness that got to me!"

Alicia stood up and paced again. "The kitten. I tried to clean it. But I could never get the smell out. It followed me everywhere. I hated it so much. I just wanted it to go away. And it did, eventually." She stopped and stared at the picture of the hovering seagull. "That gull seems higher in the air then it used to." Alicia sat down again and sighed.

"I swore I'd never let any guy ever touch me again."

"Does that apply to your husband too?" asked Doctor Ross.

"No, of course not. But if I ever met up with that bastard again..." She shook her raised fist. "When he finished he just left me tied up and gagged. I was panicky and it took me a while to struggle loose."

"Your husband wouldn't do that?" asked Doctor Ross.

"No, of course not," said Alicia.

"Did you tell your parents about the rape?"

"No way! I just put on my skirt and went home. I knew they wouldn't believe me. Look how long it took me to tell you!"

"Did you ever tell your husband about the rape?"

"No."

A week after the incident near the garage, Alicia saw Melissa playing alone in the neighbor's backyard. She seemed preoccupied as Alicia walked towards her.

"What happened to Tabby?" asked Alicia, secretly relieved.

"Who's Tabby?"

"You know, your kitten." Alicia noticed some fresh bruises on Melissa's arm.

"Oh, her. She got run over."

Inside Alicia's head the world rocked like a bird in a sudden gale of wind, buffeted from all sides.

"That's...too bad."

"What's your name?" asked Melissa.

"You...You're...kidding me. You know my name. It's Alicia."

"I'd like to get a kitten," said Melissa, her voice a monotone. She slowly raised one arm and placed it across her as though holding something. She gazed unseeingly past Alicia.

"Melissa, what's wrong?"

Melissa turned and walked toward her back door.

"Melissa!" called Alicia.

Melissa did not stop but opened the door with the same stiff motion as her automaton walk.

Alicia ran to the Smith's back door. Someone inside slammed the door. She pounded her knuckles on the door. "Answer me in there! Something's happening to your daughter!" She beat harder with her fists. "You damned fools, can't you see that?"

Still no answer. She stopped pounding and pressed her forehead against the door.

She felt a surge of pain in her swollen knuckles as she walked into her house. She was surprised to see Peter. He had returned early from his Sports Center office.

"What's going on out there?" asked Peter.

"Do you really give a damn?" replied Alicia.

"I heard a lot of noise. What happened?"

"Do you have any idea what might be going on next door?"

"Look, I don't have any idea what you're talking about..."

"Of course you don't." She leaned over toward her befuddled spouse and smelled his alcohol breath. "Did you have a good time at the Hyatt Martini Bar on the way home?"

"Actually, I came right home. Just had a one-Martini lunch with the CEO." Peter leaned forward in his chair, looked up, puzzled. "I worry about you, Alicia."

"That little girl next door is being abused. Now she's going out of her mind. That's what's going on!"

"Alicia, all I know is that you've been preoccupied the past few weeks."

"You mean I haven't wanted to have sex." Peter's silence confirmed her bull's-eye remark.

She dropped down next to Peter on the sofa, drained and numb. She wiped away a trickle of tears.

"What?" Peter looked sideways at Alicia.

"Peter, it's driving me nuts that nobody believes Melissa is being abused."

The phone rang as Alicia grappled with her tangled feelings.

"Hello," said Alicia.

"Mrs. Hammond?"

"Yes, this is Alicia Hammond."

"This is Inez Smith," her voice tremulous.

"Yes?"

"Could we talk? Maybe today?"

"Could you hold on a minute while I talk to my husband about this?" She turned to Peter and told him about the phone call.

"I think we both ought to go, Peter." Peter gave a bewildered sigh and nodded in agreement.

"My husband would like to come too if it's okay with you?" There was silence at the other end of the line. "Mrs. Smith, are you there?"

"I guess it would be okay," said Mrs. Smith. "You haven't told anyone else have you?" she added.

80

"No. We'll be right over."

Inez opened the front door to let them in. "Please come in."

"Mrs. Smith, this is my husband Peter." Alicia felt the void of Inez's greeting as Peter extended his hand for Inez's tentative handshake.

Alicia noticed more details this time: drawn brown curtains, pale-green wall-to-wall carpeting, and some padded, straight-back chairs. The off-white walls reminded her of a hospital cubicle. The family pictures looked down from high on one wall. Too high for little hands to reach. A small rust-colored couch had the secondhand look of gouges and scratches. The room looked barren without the detritus of decor, glassware, or anything fragile.

"Are you planning to buy new things for the living room?"

Inez shook her head. "No, actually we're not."

"Is Melissa here?" Alicia asked, looking around, puzzled.

"No, she's with her father. That's why I thought it would be a good time to talk." Inez smoothed one hand against the other and motioned them into the living room to sit on the couch.

"I don't know how to start." Inez resumed her hand wringing and continued to stand. "You've been interested in Melissa. She stands at the window here to notice when you come home and goes to the backyard with her cat to see if you'll come out and talk with her." Inez's forehead pinched into a V as she looked at Alicia. "For that, I'm grateful." Inez's pale-gray eyes watered. "I'm sorry." She folded her arms and sat down opposite Melissa and Peter in one of the few chairs.

"You've suspected us of abusing Melissa. You've noticed bruises on her face and arms and, lately, more of her peculiar behavior."

"Yes, I have," said Alicia. "We wanted to talk to you...or somebody about it."

"That won't be necessary." Inez sat forward, defensive. "You see, Melissa is epileptic, has been since she was a young child," said Inez, her voice unsteady. "It's just gotten worse."

"You mean all those bruises are due to epilepsy?" asked Alicia.

"No. Well, not directly. Some are due to the medicine she's taking and some are due to the violent behavior caused by the epilepsy. She sometimes picks up objects to throw or runs out of the house without warning, banging into things. That's why we have so little furniture. She wakes up during the night to run out and we try to hold her down. Sometimes we don't know where she has run to."

"Mrs. Smith, I wish we'd known. I'm glad you told me," said Alicia.

"We moved here because people in the other neighborhoods didn't take to having a violent child around their children. The real estate agent said you didn't have any children."

Inez sat back, her hands entwined, her shoulders hunched. "I suppose you're wondering why she's not here?"

"Yes," said Alicia.

"She went with her father to see a neurosurgeon about an operation that might cure her." Inez's eyes brimmed with fresh tears. "They're going to cut into her brain to get rid of her epilepsy." Inez sat up, arms folded tight around her spare body. "She is such a great little girl, easy to get along with and manage when her disease doesn't have a hold of her."

"When did you find out that Melissa had epilepsy?" asked Alicia.

"She began having small seizures when she was two years old. The doctor said she would outgrow them, but she didn't. After a while medicine didn't help much either."

Alicia pulled her hand away from Peter's and leaned forward. "How long have you been married?"

"About five years. After that my husband abandoned us, saying he wasn't going to be tied down to a sick child. That's when I met Smitty. He's been drawn to Melissa and wanted to do everything he could to make her better."

Alicia felt a prickle of anxiety. "What do they do together?"

"Well, for one thing they've spent a lot of time with cats. We've had a lot of them—calicos, even siamese and plain old alley cats."

A flush expanded on Alicia's cheeks.

"I think Smitty gets as much out of the cats as she does."

"Your new husband is very attached to both Melissa and cats then?" Alicia felt a growing lump in her throat.

"Oh, he's a good man but he's not my husband, although Melissa thinks of him as her real father. It's just that we've lived together for several years now and he's very protective of her. He's always afraid she'll be taken advantage of. He felt abandoned himself." Inez threaded her fingers together tightly, placing them in her lap "It's complicated. I've never gotten the whole story."

"The whole story?" asked Alicia. She pushed closer to the edge of the sofa as she searched for the last few pieces of a jigsaw puzzle.

"Smitty never got along with his stepfather, a man named Smith who insisted the family take his name. When his mother paid more attention to the stepfather and to her stepchildren than to him, he started running away. Finally, Smitty just left."

"So Smith is not his real name and he's called Smitty as a nickname?"

"It's from his mother's remarried name. His real name is Turner."

A wave of anxiety sucked away Alicia's breath. "Was his real first name Tommy, Tommy Turner?"

"No. That's his older brother. He's in jail now for almost beating someone to death." Inez paused to sort out a story told to her in bits and pieces. "You see, Tommy bullied Smitty. He used to strangle his pets, like his cats, gerbils, and anything Smitty loved." Inez's voice wavered. "Even shot Smitty's dog and set one of his cats on fire."

Alicia grabbed for Peter's hand.

"It's hard to understand what Smitty has been through unless you've been through it yourself," said Inez, sighing. "He wants to put it behind him, start a new life."

83

When Alicia got home, she sat by the window. It began to rain. Peter was in the next room. She could tell by his breathing that he was asleep. She slowly raised one arm and stiffly pet a kitten that was not there. She watched the rain bead on the window, joining into larger drops and running down, and thought of new beginnings.

II

Poems and Anecdotes

Sixty Together

How does sixty together sound to you?
It has the ring of longevity, blinds the eye like a shield to life.
   Only those so honored understand the stuff of life it takes.
The light tread of fate that presents itself to those who
create their path starting with a joyful meander.
   Not knowing what awaits.
It casts a thin shadow to be followed
grasped tightly and filled lightly
with experience hardened unsuspectingly
to become who you are.
   What is sixty bound together?
Only you will know
once your meandering becomes who you are.

Where Do I Fit In?

I watch the scamper of grandchildren.
   Their sideways glance.
   The glint of mischief in their eyes.
   Not ready to play the game of life untied.
I wonder not knowing the effect of graying hair, once bold,
how to seek in my mind's eye younger years.
Or should I impart well-honed but scarred wisdom?
They want to play hide and seek.
I wonder where the rudder of my life fits in with theirs.
And fear to speak.

Longevity

Oh if it be so! This overreach of old age.
As life narrows, to make added years the goal of life.
To stand aside, intrude only when called upon.
To counsel those who are headed toward the same
set-aside life.
  One in which we are stubbornly immersed,
  scurrying to catch driblets from a younger life.

Salute to Jan on Her 80th Birthday

What can you say about Jan? She is beautiful both inside and out. She doesn't walk on water but she knows where the stumps are—she is very practical. She is also very smart. I don't know who said it—I think it was Gandhi—"Live as if you were to die tomorrow. Learn as if you were to live forever." That's been her mantra.

She has had an impact on everybody in this room. So here is to Jan—my Jan, your Jan, our Jan.

Wayne Hotel
  Wayne, PA
  January 2013

Shaping Minds

Phillip was precocious early on to the point his mother and I took for granted his textbook answers to questions posed by adults. For instance, when a spinster neighbor lady told five-year-old Phillip babies came from God he promptly corrected her by saying: "No they came from a seed planted in the mother growing in an egg. When they become too big for the egg they are in a uterus. When they become too big for the uterus they get born."

About this time I began to have some slack in my busy schedule and decided to teach Phillip to play chess. In a matter of one brief session he not only mastered some complex chess piece moves but also was able to strategize openings!

Phillip often contradicted teachers in their teaching procedures. One teacher in the early grades, in order to quell his criticism and, in a state of vexation, invited him to take over her class. He calmly and successfully obliged her.

Brian, fifteen months younger than Phillip, worried us due to his lack of verbalization despite well developed motor skills. Instead he relied on Phillip to speak for him while Brian stood aside. Of course Phillip was eager to do so.

One day after months of Brian's muteness we noted an abrupt change: Brian began speaking in whole sentences and even began correcting what Phillip offered as correct! This was to be the forerunner of a lasting rivalry. At that time I noted a last parting shot at Phillip's attempt to reestablish his dominance when Brian, asking for milk, indicated he wanted a "glass of silk" to which Phillip vehemently admonished: "nilk Brian, nilk!" Though this leveled the playing field a bit, it represented Brian's struggle to step outside the shadow created by an older brother.

Both Phillip and Brian are high academic achievers and to this day Phillip's firm statement is that: "Brian is as smart as I am." Also Phillip's attitude as a highly respected professor is one of teaching others as opposed to dictating to others. This is a far cry from dictating to a younger brother by thinking for him. As Phillip says today, "I now shape minds."

Trike

When Allison was about three years old she took a trike out of the garage, one of her older brother's cast-offs, and, being a quick learner, pedaled it down the driveway into the suburban street of Hillside Way in Camillus, NY where we lived at the time.

I was coming around to the front yard and saw her across the road just as a dump truck came down the road and as she was turning to come back across the road in the path of the oncoming truck. She appeared to be looking straight across, oblivious of the truck, not turning her head toward it, still pedaling the trike back across the street when she blithely put her hand up toward the truck driver and continued to pedal across the street. The squeal of brakes was a welcome sound in obedience to Allison's traffic-cop gesture.

How do you scold a three-year-old who scared her father out of his skin? Her behavior, indeed somewhat imprudent, nevertheless imitated a classical gesture practiced by qualified adults (policemen) to control behavior. She'd seen it a number of times on TV. I decided to apply my "father knows best approach," salted down with her argument that she'd done something dangerous, but under the circumstances her behavior had been beneficent to her existence in the final analysis. My tone was mildly scolding.

Later in the day in copy of my response to the rule that she was no longer allowed to cross the street unsupervised or play in it, she went into a rant with one of her brothers, scolding him for riding the trike in the street. That behavior turned out to be the beginning of a bossy attitude towards her brothers existing to this day.

Soul Mate

Finding a Soul Mate is like pulling a chestnut out of the fire, as my grandfather always said. You know it's there somewhere, maturing to perfection, but searching for it becomes complicated, shrouded with the everyday concerns of life. When Carolyn and Bruce found the perfect chestnut in their relationship they realized it had been there all the time—just like my grandfather said it was. Finding a Soul Mate—the one who has been there all the time—is like finding the perfect chestnut nestled there, ready to be picked out at just the right time. Yes, Carolyn and Bruce have found the Soul Mate to their life together. Here's to the continuation of that journey to discover what was always there.

Waiting for Me

An ode to celebrate Meg's fiftieth birthday.

The last in line competes with sibling high achievers.
Becoming like them but being different as well.
Intelligence blooms more forcefully.
Compassion nurtured.
Life's hard knocks mastered.
The mix feeding creativity.
Becomes a mantra.
   The last one speaks:
"Mama from soft clay it is me you see.
Because you waited for me.
Your enveloping protectiveness an invisible shield.
Dadaw's scarred wisdom an added layer."

"Gramp" and Me

My grandfather Ludwig Faulhaber—called "Lud" for short but "Gramp" by me—a quiet, gentle man, more forceful than he looked, loved the movies. Almost every Friday evening, starting when I was seven years old, I would walk the mile or so with him to the only movie house in town, owned by a family whose grasping hands had a foothold into every major business in my small hometown of Hamburg, NY. My grandfather particularly liked the Friday night movies because he was partial to cowboy movies starring stalwarts such as Tom Mix and Hopalong Cassidy who invariably played in them back then. So on Friday evenings I would walk alongside my grandfather, reaching my hand out to his occasionally, his hand always there to be held.

I often wondered why he crossed the street in front of the Masonic Lodge, an imposing edifice that presided over the center of town. I found out much later that he was a mucky-muck nth degree Mason.

One particular Friday he motioned me to go inside the movie house while he paid the ten-cents fee. I heard my grandfather, at least I thought I heard him, because his voice was sharp and abrupt, unlike my grandfather's usual words of encouragement.

My grandfather then grabbed my hand so we could pick a spot in the middle of the movie house where the sound, due to some acoustical quirk, could be heard better. (My grandfather's hearing deteriorated throughout his life, an impairment I probably inherited from him.

Despite this impairment he managed a passable mastery with the trumpet that merited a place in the local fireman's parade band.)

We sat down, my grandfather more fixed on the movie than usual and his manner inscrutable. Afterward on our walk home to the corner of Haviland and Lake Streets where my grandparents lived just a few doors from us, I realized my grandfather had been continually muttering since we left the movie house—repetitive phrases and words such as "cheap," "old lady can't get enough," and chuckling "she wears a money belt attached to her garter belt."

The old lady he was referring to was indeed the grand dame of the family that practically owned the town—including the movie house—the matriarch herself who sat on a raised stool because of her short stature and sold tickets for the only movie house in town.

What my grandfather had been reacting to was the penny more he had to pay for the movie ticket due to the added tax passed on to the movie goers, rather than being absorbed by the richest family in town.

Grandfather

My hand held his
dropped down to grasp
to lead me around sidewalk spaces
and other dangerous places.
I studied his face forward
the firm wrinkled frown.
The nth degree Mason nodded
toward the temple he knew so well.
We rounded the corner
I pushed ahead first
fare in hand, his presence felt.
We entered the dark
joined hands again
the Friday night movie had so begun.

Close to the Door

A cheerful face, a smiling face.
An attitude and style—"could and would be done."
She stands close to the door.
Ready to open it to opportunity to do more.
Now we honor Wendy as we should for ever more.

Drumbeat

Has Chris been taken from us?
   We feel his smile within us.
   We hear a drumbeat too.
   The drumbeat only he can hear becomes one we hear too.
No, he has not been taken from us.
We can hear the drumbeat grow.
No, he has not left us.
We feel and hear him too.

Space

My friend's wife died.
The work of grieving begun a distance from my own.
He gathers friends and family around him.
A blanket to repel an unaccompanied life.
  Stepping towards him an imbalance felt.
A chord of remembrance strikes his eyes.
Needing time to sort it out if he cares to share it at all.
  I wait as he sets the pace.
I step away to leave space for a grieving yet to come.
As my friend assembles remnants from his deserted life.

Limbo

Penultimate wine enfeebles balance.
Swaying to kaleidoscopic colors in the back bar mirror.
Weaving towards the revolving door.
Thoughts in suspension like
an adolescent with new found atheism.
Yet unsure.
Retreating to a limbo.
Pondering the next move.
What shall it be?
The manager like a shepherd comes fore.
Guides the way through the door.
As he has done for the wayward scores of times before.

Times

My desk clock tells time in a world requiring exactness.
Knowing eternity awaits there is not time but times.
Time did not respect Pickett's order
to face bone shattering cannon.
No hint of turning back.
No one to receive Lee's accepted blame.
The armless Venus reigns resolute on the desk
with the mud colored cannon ball.
The contrast stings.
To what end the order given a wise man would dispute?
Venus bears witness to her time. Her beauty flawed.
So does the Gettysburg cannon ball remind.
A simple address by a flawed giant of a man.

The Angler's Lure

Arrogant white plumage
settling onto shimmering ripples
riding atop, seeking swifter currents
unlimited worlds to conquer
Magellan sailing through the strait
inattentive to the unexpected
ruin for one not sensed by the other
tailing away to meet fate another day.

Critter

When I picked up the critter he balled up. I could hardly do it he was so tiny. When I left him alone he turned into a longer critter and I let him crawl across my hand. It tickled like my favorite nanny blanket. The critter moved around a lot. I didn't have to move him like I do my Hoppity Beanie Rabbit.

I wanted to keep him but Grandpa said I should put him back where I found him in the grass. When I cried Grandpa said I could keep him if we put him in a cup but not cover him so he couldn't breathe. Grandpa said the critter can't see but knows where he is going because of the feelers in his head. He said the feelers are called antennae.

We just moved here and Grandpa is already visiting us. Daddy said it's a nice place and there'll be new kids. But Brendan won't be here. He had to stay. I'll miss him. Brendan's mother wouldn't let him go with us. We could've taken care of him but Daddy said Brendan wanted to be with his Mommy and Daddy. But our Mommy and Daddy could've helped take care of him, right? Anyway, Ryan said he didn't care whether Brendan had come with us or not. He's already found a friend here named Freddie. He told me about his new friend but I've never seen him. I don't think he really has a friend. He just says he does.

I'm glad Grandpa is already visiting us. He's funny. He has things in his ears that whistle when you put your hands over them. He said he needs them so he can hear better. He likes to put his hat on me. When he does I run and he chases me. Sometimes his glasses fall down his nose when he runs after me. I would rather play hide-and-seek with Grandpa more than anyone else because I like it when he finds me. Ryan cries when Grandpa finds him.

Mommy wanted me to put the critter back in the grass too. I cried a lot about that. I told her I could take care of the critter and that the critter didn't need his Mommy and Daddy. We would be his Mommy and Daddy.

I kept the critter in the toy room and let it crawl over Ryan's train station. That made Ryan mad. He said he would run over the critter with his train. I think he was mad because I have a critter and he doesn't.

I lost the critter for a while. I didn't know where it had crawled. I knew I had to find him. That was my critter. Mommy was mad because I jumped up and down about it.

Grandpa said there were other critters, but I told him this critter was special and it didn't need anybody but me. I cried again but I didn't jump up and down. I told Grandpa the critter was special because I found him while I was with him. Grandpa said maybe the critter was a grandpa and was looking for his grandchildren. I said that the critter didn't look that old to me. Grandpa said critters don't show their age but that doesn't mean they don't have grandchildren.

Grandpa finally found the critter. I asked Grandpa whether the critter got lost because he couldn't hear good. Grandpa said that might be and so maybe we ought to put the critter where he could find his grandchildren with his feelers. I said maybe they even hug with their feelers. Grandpa said that may be so too.

We took the critter to the backyard where it could hide in the grass and under rocks. I told Grandpa that I hope all grandpa critters find their grandchildren. Ryan said he hoped so too.

Hello Caroline

Hello Caroline,

Here is my response to the questions that you posed to me about veterans and remembrance. I will follow pretty close to the format that you gave me with your questions.

I was 17 years old when I enlisted in the army in September, 1946. I needed my parents consent to do so and joined primarily to pay for my college education through the GI Bill of Rights (my discharge date was July 1948 as a Sergeant). I was assigned to the Army Ordinance and after Basic Training, while stationed at Aberdeen, MD, I was trained to be an Instrument Repairman, especially for watches (they were the old complicated type essential to coordinate battle). I also learned how to use various weapons and drive a tank (I didn't have a driver's license before I enlisted, so learned how to drive a tank before I learned how to drive a car!).

After my training in the States I was shipped to Okinawa, a part of southern Japan, early 1947 as part of the Occupation Forces. This island was to be the jumping off invasion area to conquer Japan proper but with the dropping of the atomic bomb in August, 1945, it became unnecessary. So fortunately for me I never participated in any battle but saw some of its aftereffects on the Japanese people who were still very scared of the Americans. Many killed themselves to avoid us. In the three month battle starting April 1945, the Americans lost about 40,000 killed or wounded (15,000 killed) in the bloodiest battle in US history. However the Japanese army was completely wiped out—108,000 killed in the 3 months the battle raged.

I had many friends in the service from various parts of the US, all the way from Georgia crackers to salmon fisherman from Oregon. I visited China with some of them and we all gradually got to know that the Japanese and Chinese are very fine people. One of them was our Sergeants Club bartender who was an ex Japanese colonel who escaped being killed by us by blending into the Okinawan population. Another was Suzy, a well educated Japanese woman who was our base librarian.

I don't hear much from my GI buddies anymore, primarily because my army enlistment was only 2 years and there were constant changes of personnel. There wasn't the same bonding that is so intense between soldiers who are fighting for their lives. Besides, I had a whole college life ahead of me that shaped my relationships and even thought about going to college on a football scholarship through my football playing while on Okinawa (yes football was a big sport on the island and helped diminish the boredom).

You ask about people I lived with and I've mentioned both the GIs as well as the civilian population. There is another factor that fits in with who I was stationed with and that is the racial and gender separation. Despite the sentiment towards integration by race it simply had not taken effect in the Army when I was in the service and was completely unheard of in regard to gender. It was much later that racial integration officially took effect and still later that gender integration did.

You asked me whether any of my experiences changed me and I can only say I began to realize that people the world over and the society they live in are more similar than they are different and that people want to be different but not rejected because they are different. (That's a mouthful, I know, but think about it.)

War is a waste of human beings and can be avoided if we involve the world, literally empower the countries of the world to resolve disputes before they escalate out of control. I'm thinking along the lines, for instance, of developing a more effective governing body such as the U.N. regarding the use of weapons.

Caroline, I hope this helps you understand a bit about how my experiences as a soldier shaped the way I think today. I'd be glad to discuss further.

Looking forward to seeing you soon.

Love,
Grandpa

The Perfect Chestnut

Musings From a Meandering Psychiatrist, or How Psychiatry Became Part of My Life:

Life has ways of pulling you in directions you don't want to go. This often has been the fate of anyone who deals with the human condition. It's like pulling chestnuts out of the fire—you know the chestnut kept in the fire at a certain temperature will have a perfect taste even though one risks being burned in the process of attempting to achieve that perfect taste and, after all, how can one know what a perfect chestnut tastes like since a perfect chestnut is unknown. We know perfection exists somewhere even though we don't know what it is. We just know it is often subject to the vagaries of thought, emotion, and arbitration.

You may call it life, I call it meandering toward perfection.

Searching

Isolated water under a grey splintered bridge.
Crossing to another pasture.
Looking down.
Cleaving fin.
Disrupting concentric ripples.
Between two worlds.
One yet to be found.
Searching.

About the Author

Dr. Gene Cary is a retired psychiatrist living with his wife Jan in Hershey, PA where they raised their five children. Dr. Cary graduated and later became a faculty member of the Department of Psychiatry at the State University of New York (SUNY) at Syracuse, N.Y. He then moved to Hershey where he helped develop and direct the Department of Psychiatry at the Penn State University Milton Hershey Medical Center. He later carried on a varied psychiatric practice that included teaching, consulting, and forensic work. Retirement from an active practice gave him the opportunity to develop his interest in creative writing, and he switched from writing articles about psychiatry to writing fiction and poetry.